LAST MINUTE

College
Financing

It's Never Too Late to Plan for the Future

by Daniel J. Cassidy

CAREER
PRESS

Franklin Lakes, NJ

BRIGHTON PUBLIC LIBRARY
999 BRIGHTON ROAD
TONAWANDA, NEW YORK 14150
LB 2337.4 .C396 2000
0000192074847

Copyright © 2000 by National Scholarship Research Service, a
division of Cassidy Research Corporation

All rights reserved under the Pan-American and International Copyright Conventions. This book may not be reproduced, in whole or in
part, in any form or by any means electronic or mechanical, including
photocopying, recording, or by any information storage and retrieval
system now known or hereafter invented, without written permis-
sion from the publisher, The Career Press.

LAST MINUTE COLLEGE FINANCING
Cover design by Foster & Foster
Printed in the U.S.A. by Book-mart Press

To order this title, please call toll-free 1-800-CAREER-1 (NJ and
Canada: 201-848-0310) to order using VISA or MasterCard, or for
further information on books from Career Press.

CAREER
PRESS

The Career Press, Inc., 3 Tice Road, PO Box 687,
Franklin Lakes, NJ 07417
www.careerpress.com

Library of Congress Cataloging-in-Publication Data

Cassidy, Daniel J., 1956-
    Last minute college financing : it's never too late to plan for the future /
by Daniel J. Cassidy.
        p.   cm.
    Includes index.
    ISBN 1-56414-468-2 (paper)
    1. Student aid—United States. 2. Education, Higher—United States—
Finance. I. Title.

LB2337.4. C396 2000
378.3'0973—dc21   00-031212

NOV 1 3 2000

#4394S264
34

I wish to thank all of those who have made *Last Minute College Financing* possible. My sincere thanks and gratitude go to:

Shawn Lindstrom, Assistant Director of Financial Aid at Ithaca College in New York for the Government Aid section

and

the staff at NSRS, especially:

my wife, Deirdre Carlin Cassidy, Vice President/Controller

Research and Computer Engineering department heads Tammy M. Parnell and Richard E. Merwin

Administration and Public Relations department heads Jean E. Van Dyke and Joseph D. Gargiulo

A very special thank you to Jim Eason of ABC's KGO & KSFO Radio, San Francisco, the man who made NSRS possible

---

and Larry King for taking NSRS national!

Finally, my sincere thanks to the staff of Career Press, especially, Ron Fry, President and Publisher, for their hard work and support.

Contents

T

he Last Minute Guide to College Financing is a how-to guide and information resource on paying for higher education. The world of financial aid is broken up into two main categories, the private sector, and the government. Because these two arenas are so different, this guide has a separate section devoted to each one. I hope that the information provided here will help enrich your understanding of the financial aid process and will guide you in your planning of a higher education. Good Luck!

—Daniel J. Cassidy, President and Founder
National Scholarship Research Service

The National Scholarship Research Service (NSRS) Story

When I began my college career, I went to the college financial aid office, like most students in need of financial aid. I needed some sort of financial aid because I had an agreement with my parents: They would pay my room and board at any school I wanted to attend, but I had to pay the tuition. Unfortunately, my Scholastic Aptitude Test (SAT) scores weren't good enough for me to get into a state school, where the tuition was relatively inexpensive. Luckily, I did qualify to attend University of San Francisco (USF), but that meant I would have to come up with $5,000 a year for tuition! Not only would I need to work summers, I would have to get really involved with financial aid. I was surprised to learn that, at that time, 80 percent of all students relied on some form of financial aid. That is still true today.

I also learned that 50 percent of all students that dropped out of college listed financial difficulty as the number one reason for doing so. In high school, I hadn't prepared for financial aid. I had been more concerned about where I was going to go to college and how I was going to get in. So my introduction to financial aid began in my freshman year at USF.

At the University's financial aid office, I was given information about state and federal money and a list of school endowments, which are scholarships that the college itself administers and that are given by alumni and local businesses. USF was fortunate in this regard, because many businesses and individuals had contributed money for buildings, scholarships, and school equipment. Among them were Mrs. Dean Witter of the investment firm Dean Witter, Mrs. Davies of Davies Hospital, San Francisco, Calif., and Ben Swigg, the owner of the world-famous Fairmont Hotel. They donated money not only for buildings, but also for scholarships in specific fields of study.

Fortunately, the USF financial aid office let me know about those endowments. Many schools don't provide that information unless you ask for it. Be sure to use your financial aid office; it's a service you are paying for. Your financial aid office also will have information about a wide spectrum of financial aid, including military/ROTC scholarships, athletic scholarships and contests, festivals, and awards in the arts. You should meet with a financial aid counselor at least once a year—if not every semester—in order to stay on top of government and private endowments.

After learning about government aid and private endowments at the financial aid office, I started thinking about private sector sources. Some common organizations that came to mind were Rotary, Lions Club, Elks, and Zonta International. I went to the library thinking there might be a book on the subject. This was 1975 and, back then, Macmillan Publishing's *College Blue Book,* still in print today, listed about 1,200 sources. To my surprise, not only were common private sector sources listed, but I found many others that I had never thought of. Hughes Aircraft, Shell Oil, sororities, fraternities, and clubs, for example, all offered educational benefits. Essentially, the book listed all five categories that make up private sector sources: corporations, trusts, memorials, foundations, and religious groups.

I wrote to some of the sources and requested their scholarship applications. When I began receiving responses, I realized the applications were quite easy to fill out, usually one to two pages in length and very similar to each other in form. Most required an essay, some an interview; thus, my involvement in the private sector scholarship arena began.

By applying to these private sector sources each year and still using the USF financial aid office, I was able to complete my degrees in international business and pre-med at USF, spend a summer studying at Yale, and graduate with my master's degree in chemistry. Then I enrolled at University of California San Francisco (UCSF) School of Medicine, where I began a doctoral program in pathology. By that time, I had acquired almost $20,000 in private sector scholarships — a big deal back then.

At UCSF, I received some more scholarships from the private sector and began my lab work in collagen biochemistry in breast cancer. About that time (1980), the federal government's Health Education Assistance Loans (HEAL) program was cut back. This program supplied financial aid to the health sciences. Nursing, medical, and dental students all were eligible for assistance until the cutbacks. A lot of my friends and student colleagues worried that they wouldn't be able to continue their education without HEAL program funds. They asked how I had received scholarships for UCSF and how they could go about obtaining funding. I told them about the scholarships I had received from the private sector. Fortunately, I had saved all the information that I had collected during my four years of research at UCSF.

I told my friends to go ahead and use it. At the time, I had about 2,000 scholarship sources in my research files.

Being an impoverished doctoral student, I decided that I might be able to earn a few dollars by putting my research information into a computer and matching the specific students to the scholarships that had been stored in two file drawers. My idea was fairly simple and it wasn't particularly difficult for me since I had just finished working on a computer program that matched medical students to hospitals for their internships. I sent out a news release to local television and radio stations, newspapers, and magazines.

At that time, the Apple II computer was coming into widespread use and a popular talk-show host, Jim Eason at KGO radio, had just purchased one. He saw our news release and was interested in talking to us about how the computer was matching students to scholarships. My wife and I went on the air and talked for an hour about how lucrative the private sector was, and how different it was compared to traditional forms of financial aid. I remember that Mr. Eason kept asking me if I was sure I would be able to handle the response the radio show would generate. "No problem," I assured him. To my surprise, we received more than 3,000 letters that week requesting the scholarship matching service. Thus, National Scholarship Research Service (NSRS) was born. I had accidentally stubbed my toe on a need and I've been filling it ever since.

I continued using the same format during our early years: doing talk shows that told students and parents about the private sector funding sources and providing the NSRS scholarship search service that enabled students to locate those sources. Then, in 1984, we decided to put our information into a book format. The result was *The Scholarship Book* with Prentice Hall. It has fostered two offshoots published by Career Press: *The Worldwide Graduate Scholarship Directory* and *The Worldwide College Scholarship Directory*. The books are an inexpensive way to disseminate the information to students who would rather spend less money and do their own research.

For those students who wish to hire a professional search service, there are several benefits: The scholarship search service offered by NSRS, for example, includes Scholarship Alert(sm) with automatic notification, where NSRS contacts the scholarship sources for you. Updates (offered for a fee) are recommend on an annual basis because even the student's age can make a difference in the scholarship opportunities. The scholarship search service saves you time and lends tremendous accuracy to your scholarship research. Also, the information from the computerized service is more current because of the ability to update information almost immediately.

While doing your search, you also want to be aware of scholarship search service scams. Parents and students should avoid any service that guarantees a scholarship award or that offers any monetary awards. (See Chapter 1 for a more detailed discussion of scams.)

Why all the fuss?

Today, the $20,000 in scholarships that I was awarded might buy a year at most colleges. The cost of a public university ranges from $5,000 to $10,000 per year. A private school costs $10,000 to more than $20,000 per year. Many families clearly have a need for financial aid. And because it is available, you shouldn't think you have to limit your dreams simply because you don't have the financial resources in your bank account. There is help. Now you just have to match your needs with what's available.

Thousands of students have paid for their college education with government scholarships, school endowments, and private sector funding. Today, students are receiving outrageous amounts of money. For example, in 1992, Marianne "Angel" Ragins from Macon, Ga., was offered more than $300,000 in scholarships. She applied for many private sector scholarships using one of my directories, and she found that getting them just wasn't that difficult. When she appeared on ABC's *Good Morning America,* she reiterated the same point I had made on the show a week earlier: Scholarship awards are not always based on income or grades; deadlines are daily and age is not a restriction. She chose a scholarship package that included a four-year full ride at Florida A&M, a computer for use in her room, and a summer trip to Austria, totaling more than $120,000. That's a record for sure!

Let's get started

So, there you have it — how NSRS was started. I had a need, like most college students do, especially today, with the costs continuing to rise. And as you can see, I didn't let that stop me. By doing some digging — some of it not all that deep — I was able to find sources that would help me fulfill my college dreams. And along the way, I found that I could put that information to good use, and help thousands of other students who are just like I was. All you have to do is get started. So let's do it!

Part I

The Private Sector

Chapter 1

Financial Aid and Scholarship Opportunities

Before we get into the details of searching for scholarships, the application process, and all that lies ahead, let's take a minute to review some trends in private sector philanthropy.

The facts

Philanthropy in this country is alive and well. From 1982 to 1997, charitable donations increased an average of 14 percent each year. If we look at overall philanthropy in the United States (which includes everything from Jerry's Kids for Muscular Dystrophy to The United Way), we see that since 1982, philanthropy in this country has increased 5.6 times. Take a look at the following table:

Table 1: Growth in Philanthropy 1982-1997			
Year	Overall Philanthropy (in billions)[1]	% Increase	Educational Funding (in billions)[2]
1982	$58.67	—	$8.80
1983	$67.87	16%	$10.18
1984	$74.05	9%	$11.11
1985	$102.06	38%	$15.31
1987	$115.44	13.11%	$17.32
1988	$122.08	6%	$18.31
1989	$137.54	13%	$20.63
1990	$142.48	4%	$21.37
1991	$162.91	14%	$24.44
1992	$176.82	9%	$26.52
1993	$189.21	7%	$28.38
1994	$195.79	4%	$29.37
1995	$226.74	14%	$34.01
1996	$267.58	16%	$40.14
1997	$329.91	19%	$49.49

(1) Source: *Foundation Giving: Yearbook of Facts and Figures on Private, Corporate, and Community Foundations* by Loren Renz and Steven Lawrence (New York: The Foundation Center, 1995), p. 10. Figures for 1986 are not available.

(2) Source: *The Chronicle of Philanthropy,* April 1990, reports that an average 15% of philanthropic giving is devoted to scholarships, fellowships, grants, and other moneys for postsecondary education.

This growth is due primarily to increased stock performance in late 1989 and an increase in giving from individuals. When we think of philanthropy, we usually think of large foundations, such as Ford, Rockefeller, or Kellogg. The fact is, 83 percent of overall philanthropy in the United States comes from individuals — people like you and me.

More than 15 percent of overall philanthropy goes toward educational funding (see Table 1). This translates to about $49 billion that is available from the private sector for scholarships, fellowships, grants, and loans — and this is just in the United States. The international arena is just as lucrative. At National Scholarship Research Service (NSRS), we have tracked another $30 billion in international funds from Australia to Zimbabwe, bringing the worldwide total to some $79 billion.

To give you another perspective, 54 percent of today's financial aid for college comes from the private sector. Just as the financial aid office doesn't always advertise endowments bequeathed to the school, the private sector doesn't always make known the availability of its scholarships. It's up to you to get involved, do your research, and send in your application.

The National Commission on Student Financial Assistance and the House Subcommittee on Postsecondary Education found that more than one-third of available funds goes unclaimed each year — not because students don't qualify, but because they don't know that the money is available, and thus, don't apply. A study performed by the American Association of Fund Raising Council reported that 80 percent of all applications to some 44,000 private foundations were either filled out incorrectly or were misdirected. In 1992, NSRS found that $2.7 billion went undistributed. This demonstrates the gap between available funds and the knowledge of their existence. There is an evident need for making students aware of what is available to them and then putting them in touch with the proper scholarship sources. That's where scholarship services and books, such as those offered by NSRS, can be valuable tools.

Another reason these scholarships go unclaimed is because of the inaccurate interpretation and misapplication of old rules. Some guidelines that applied to government sources of aid were incorrectly believed to pertain to the private sector. Many of these misconceptions originated as restrictions or rules with state and federal scholarships, and now it is not uncommon that students fail to apply for private sector scholarships because they think these restrictions apply here as well. Such old standard exclusionary sayings as "my parents earn too much money"; "my grades are not good enough"; "the deadlines are only in the fall"; or "I am too old to get a scholarship" do not apply to scholarships offered in the private sector. If anything, the opposite is true.

For example:

- ⏱ **Financial need** is not a top requirement of 80 percent of the scholarships offered in the private sector. Most private sector sources don't care how much money a student's parents make. The 20 percent that do care have a wide variety of qualifying ranges.

- ⏱ **Grades** aren't always the most important factor; 90 percent of the private sector is not looking for the straight-A student. Sometimes a student can get a scholarship just by going through an interview, promising to work for a company afterward, or simply filling out an application. Everything from personal, occupational, and educational background and goals can lead to a scholarship.

- ⏱ **Deadlines**, quite literally, pass every day. Anytime is a good time to get involved in the process. Deadlines may be set up to fit the offering corporation's tax year or they may simply be set up for the convenience of the group that meets to review the scholarship applications.

- ⏱ **Age** is not always a restriction. In 1990, one out of four students in the United States was over the age of 25. Today, almost half of all students are over 25. Many students are parents finishing degrees after starting families. Others are making career changes as we shift from the industrial wave to the high-tech arena. Still others are students who have postponed college until they could afford it. There are many, many scholarship sources interested in mid-career development students.

College saving and scholarship preparation

During my radio interviews, many students and parents ask me when they should start looking for scholarships. I always answer, "As soon as possible." Getting involved in financial aid and financial planning obviously can keep you from pushing the panic button at the last minute. But as I said before, deadlines come up every day, and if you are *really* getting started at the last minute, apply for those scholarships immediately.

To give you an ideal scenario, I have prepared a College Planning Timeline (pages 26 to 27). Beginning right during a child's elementary school years, both parents and student should be thinking about college in some way, whether it be setting up a special savings account, finding scholarship sources, or taking the right classes so as to not have to take — and pay for — them at the college level. Regardless of where on the timeline you are beginning, refer to it to stay on track.

Ideally, parents should begin saving when their child is a toddler. By setting up a monthly savings plan that is affordable for your household, you can begin building a fund for your child's college education immediately.

Table 2: How Much College Will Cost You, and the Monthly Savings Needed to Pay for It					
Years to College	School Year Fall	Projected 4-Year Total Cost (Public)	Projected 4-Year Total Cost (Private)	Monthly Savings (Public)	Monthly Savings (Private)
1	2000	50,239	106,895	1,231	2,620
2	2001	52,751	112,240	930	1,979
3	2002	55,389	117,852	749	1,593
4	2003	58,158	123,745	628	1,336
5	2004	61,066	129,932	541	1,151
6	2005	64,120	136,428	476	1,012
7	2006	67,326	143,250	425	904
8	2007	70,692	150,412	384	817
9	2008	74,226	157,933	350	745
10	2009	77,938	165,830	322	685
11	2010	81,835	174,121	298	634
12	2011	85,296	182,827	277	590
13	2012	90,223	191,968	259	551
14	2013	94,734	201,567	243	517
15	2014	99,470	211,645	229	487
16	2015	104,444	222,228	216	487
17	2016	109,666	233,339	205	435
18	2017	115,150	245,006	194	413

If you are in this position and are starting early, NSRS has a table called EduSave that can help. It is a college savings plan for parents of small children. The typical EduSave scenario goes like this: You put away a specific amount every month, depending on the cost of your child's school of choice. If you're saving for a public institution, $194 per month should be sufficient. If you're saving for a private college, you will have to more than double that to $413 per month. The $194 savings plan for a state-supported college would represent an out-of-pocket cost to you of about $2,328 per year. With simple or higher interest accruing (of between 5 and 6 percent), you would have about $115,150 available for your child's college education at the end of the 20-year

Table 3: Potential Earnings of a College Graduate		
Potential Earnings	Annual Family Income	Total Earnings at age 65
College Graduate	$67,300	$2,692,000
High School Graduate	$37,100	$1,484,000
Elementary School only	$20,500	$820,000

Source: National College Resource Association

period. For a private school, that figure would more than double.

Currently, the cost of college is rising at twice the rate of inflation. As a matter of fact, in the past 10 years alone, it has increased 146 percent. Back in 1980, an article in *Money* magazine predicted it would cost almost $100,000 to send a child to college in 1990. I didn't believe it; unfortunately, it was an accurate prediction. If you look at such universities as Stanford, Harvard, or Yale, you will see that it will easily cost you more than $20,000 per year. In addition, it's taking most students more than four years to finish college.

Colleges differ in the ways they charge tuition. Some colleges, especially private universities, tend to charge a flat fee for all full-time students, regardless of how many units they are taking, and smaller fees for fewer units. Others, especially community colleges, base tuition on the number of units taken and charge a per-unit fee rather than a flat fee. When you are deciding how much of a course load to carry, keep in mind that most financial aid sources, both private and government assistance, require enrollment in *at least six units* to receive assistance.

Paying for college is probably the biggest expenditure you'll make, perhaps even more costly than buying a house. Table 2 shows you how much money you need to be saving each

Table 4: Breakdown of Total Costs		
	Private	**Public**
Tuition & Fees	$14,508	$3,243
Books & Supplies	$667	$662
Room & Board	$5,765	$4,530
Transportation	$547	$612
Personal Expenses	$1,046	$1,411
Total Costs	**$22,533**	**$10,458**

month to be able to pay for school. But what comprises these amounts? Tuition, fees, books, supplies, room and board, transportation, and even parking are all expenses students must consider. Table 4 breaks down an example of these costs.

Applying early

For the student who is looking for scholarships, I advise both student and parents to start applying for financial aid in the student's freshman year of high school. Now, this may seem early, but it really isn't. Believe it or not, there are application deadlines for college scholarships throughout each of a student's four years of high school. There are even some scholarships for seventh and eighth graders. There are more than 36,000 scholarships available for high school students, starting with 1,700 that are available just for freshmen, and doubling each year thereafter. Given the thousands of opportunities that are out there, the average student should be dealing with 20 to 30 scholarship sources each year for which they are specifically eligible.

Work as a team

I am always surprised when students put together their financial aid package during their freshman year in college, and then stop looking or applying for aid. What about the remaining years of college? Scholarships should be researched and applied for on a yearly basis. And it should be a joint effort involving both student and parents. Parents can lend a hand with the detailed financial issues and questions because of their years of experience dealing with such matters, while the student worries about other important issues like what college they will go to, how they are going to get in, what they will major in, and of course, what to wear to the prom.

Make searching for financial aid a team effort. *The plan is really very simple: Be organized, be neat, and don't procrastinate.*

Selecting schools

In order to plan for college expenses, you need to know how large — or small — those expenses will be. You can rely on tuition cost averages to a certain degree. But at some point, you need to have a tangible figure as a goal. A good place to start is by examining your choices of schools to get a realistic idea of the costs you are facing. Then you can figure out how much aid you will need to apply for.

Parents and student should sit down during the student's freshman year in high school and select possible colleges. To help with decision-making, I recommend that you invest in a good guide to four-year colleges. There are several that can be found in the reference section of your favorite bookstore. These inexpensive guides list all four-year, two-year, and vocational-technical schools in the country and should stimulate the student's interest in where to

COLLEGE PLANNING TIMELINE

K-6th grade: Talk to your children about going to college. As they get older, let them know the importance of a higher education. They should grow up expecting to attend college. Start a savings account for them and add to it monthly.

7th-8th grade: Make sure your child takes the right classes. Most courses that colleges require can be taken only after completing more basic courses. If students don't plan properly, there won't be time to complete these preliminary courses in high school and they will have to spend the extra time and money doing so in college. Middle and junior high school students should be taking:

- algebra, geometry, and other challenging math classes
- English, science, and history
- foreign language
- computer science
- the arts

Keep adding to that savings account. Discuss with your children the financial aspect of attending college. Start planning how you will pay for it. Also start thinking about the student's interests and what careers he or she may be interested in pursuing. If they show an interest in a specific field, take them to meet someone with that occupation so they can ask questions and see what the day-to-day aspect of that job entails.

9th-10th grade: Students should continue with challenging college-prep courses and get involved in extracurricular activities. They should also begin preparing for college admissions exams, such as the SAT and ACT, which need to be taken during the junior or senior year in high school. There are many books and sample exams that can help prepare students. Students may also look into Advanced Placement courses. These are college-level courses that may transfer as college credit, saving time and money.

Begin your search for scholarships. Browse through the *Worldwide College Scholarship Directory* (Career Press) and *The Scholarship Book* (Prentice Hall) to see which awards are available to high school students at any level. There are many science projects, essay competitions, art contests, etc., to which 9th and 10th graders may apply.

Have your children visit with their school counselor to make sure they are on the right track. He or she can help them plan their schedule with important classes and electives that may help them decide on a college major. Select possible colleges.

11th grade: Students should take the SAT or ACT tests. Request college catalogs to see begin narrowing down choices and to see what kind of financial aid is offered. Intensify your search for scholarships. Students should do volunteer work and/or internships in areas of interest.

12th grade: Narrow your college search down to a few choices and apply during early admission. Continue applying for scholarships (including the FAFSA). Students should retake the SAT or ACT to improve scores and take AP tests. Remember, some schools and foundations wait to make their decisions until they have the final grade report. If your child isn't accepted to any of the colleges to which he or she applied, try others in the later admission period. If this doesn't work out, a junior college is an excellent option to improve your grades and save some money, and universities are more likely to accept transfer students.

go to school. Using these books, you can cross-reference the schools via major, fields of study, geographic location, and many other helpful categories. I suggest you and your child select 10 to 15 schools and write to them to request a financial aid package, college catalog, and an admissions package. In the financial aid package, you will find all the information on state and federal funding (or you can call the U.S. Department of Education at (800)433-3243 for financial aid information). You will also find the list of endowments in most college catalogs in the financial aid section. But do your own research, too. Don't assume things haven't changed since that catalog was last printed. There may be additional sources or changes you may not find out about unless you ask.

Am I too late? Hardly.

What if you've just graduated from high school, and you're strapped for the cash needed to pay for school? Relax; you have time. All of the tips mentioned in this book still apply to you. You can still search and apply for funding, but

FOR YOUR INFORMATION...

A handy reference you might want to consider using is the *Occupational Outlook Handbook*. It lists virtually every career field—from aeronautics to zoology. It will help students consider a career path and a major field of study for college. It lists the best courses to take and the salary expectations for each occupation. I was given this book when I was 18. It was a wonderful gift that really got me thinking about what I was going to do with my life. It is published by the U.S. Department of Labor and can be ordered by calling CFKR Career Materials at (800)525-5626.

you may also want to consider some alternatives. Often, you can fill out a form to hold your place in the university while you take a semester or two off. During this period, you can get a full-time job, and put the majority of your earnings into a savings account. Then you can start school knowing you have the funds available and you can study without worry. And if you're lucky enough to get a job in a field you are seriously considering for your future, you've just gotten some real world experience that will look great on your resume. It's important to remember to try and turn what may seem like a negative into a positive situation.

Another cash-saving alternative is to attend your local community college for a couple of years. Just because it's a junior college doesn't mean it's not quality education. Admission for state residents is less expensive, and it will allow you time to save up the funds you'll need for university tuition. Additionally, it is easier for transfer students to be accepted into a university than it is for entering freshmen, and it gives you time to build and/or maintain a high grade point average (GPA). Another benefit of attending a junior college first is that you can get all of your general education requirements taken care of. Then, once you go to the university, you can concentrate on your major — and you've had two years to determine what your major will be!

Scams

As you search for funding to attend school, you must beware of services looking to take advantage of you. Make sure you check out any service you are considering using.

A disturbing number of scholarship sponsoring organizations have reported that they receive a high volume of inquiries from students who are unqualified for the awards about which they are asking.

Because of the number of these types of reports, investigations are being conducted to determine the origins of the misguided inquiries. Most often we find that someone has taken *only* names and addresses from our scholarship books and is selling the information—a general listing of scholarships available in a particular field of study—to students without regard to the student's qualifications. Most of these "rip-off operations" make no effort to match the student's educational goals and personal background with the requirements of the scholarships.

The books that we publish, for example, contain 40 tables along with the source description, providing accurate cross-matching of the student's characteristics to the requirements of scholarship sources. NSRS and the publishers of our books are doing all we can to stop any abuse of our copyright that might result in an inconvenience to our scholarship sponsoring organizations. We've assisted the Federal Trade Commission in closing down one such rip-off operation and we are currently pursuing six others.

FOR YOUR INFORMATION...

Many students believe that when they graduate high school, they are graduate students. But when you are seeking your first degree, either a two-year associate's degree, or a four-year bachelor's degree (Bachelor's of Arts or Bachelor's of Science), you are an undergraduate. Once you have received your B.A./B.S. degree, you are then considered a graduate student. These are the master's and doctoral levels of study for a professional degree. Post-master's and post-doctoral scholars may continue their education through postgraduate research projects. Scholarships from the private sector are available for all of these different levels of study.

Lastly, if any scholarship service guarantees a scholarship, savings bond, or even a fountain pen, buyer beware! If it sounds too good to be true, then it probably is. Because it is solely at the discretion of the scholarship sponsoring organizations to choose their scholarship recipients each year, these scholarship search scams cannot guarantee that users of their service will get a scholarship.

These scam techniques do not apply solely to the information provided in books or by standard search services. The increasing use of the Internet has opened a world of possibility for deception of unsuspecting victims. The same rules apply here: Investigate every search company or service you plan on using.

Let's review

Well, you've learned some history, discovered your options, and narrowed your school choices. Now it's time to start on your scholarship and financial aid search. Before you move on, let's go over some important points to get you started on the right foot.

Remember to refer to scholarship directories to help you with your search. As mentioned, my books *The Scholarship Book* (Prentice Hall) and the *Worldwide College Scholarship Directory* (Career Press), both for undergraduates, and the *Worldwide Graduate Scholarship Directory* (Career Press), for master's, doctorate, and post-doctorate levels, will help. You will find tables in the beginning of the books that will enable you to cross-reference your search by categories: educational, occupational, and personal background and goals. Computerized searches, like the one offered by NSRS, for example, do the same, although more thoroughly, but without all the effort that the books require.

Make use of all available resources, including your school's financial aid officer, counselor, and librarian. Local businesses and organizations are possible sources of funding. Your chamber of commerce or your bank manager are also good places to start. Even friends, teachers, employers, and local service clubs (such as Rotary, Lions, and Kiwanis) may be helpful, too. Look everywhere; you never know where a scholarship may be offered.

Now you're ready to begin the search process. Remember to keep your options — and your eyes — open as you look for funding sources.

Good luck!

Chapter 2

The Application Process

Now the real work begins. There are a few things you need to do to prepare for when the search gets underway. You want to be ready for the onslaught of information you are going to receive from the various scholarship sources you will contact. You might want to consider making three financial aid boxes, either out of old boxes you have around the house or plastic storage boxes, to collect and coordinate your information. Label them according to the general source: The Government Funding Box; The School Endowments Box; and The Private Sector Box. Following is a suggestion of how to organize your materials.

⏱ **The Government Funding Box.** Put all the information from the state and federal programs in this box. Keep the following phone number readily available, either by including it on

33

the label or printing it on a bright sheet of paper and attaching it to a box flap or lid: Department of Education: (800)433-3243. The Coordinating Board for your state is in your phone book under the heading "Government."

🕐 **The School Endowments Box.** Keep all alumni and local business scholarship information (which is usually listed in the financial aid section of the colleges' catalogs) in this box. Keep the catalogs in this box, too.

🕐 **The Private Sector Box.** This box should contain material you have gleaned from various scholarship directories or any scholarship search services you use, as well as information that you collect from any private sector source to which you apply.

I will talk about each of these boxes in more detail in the next section. So, now that you're organized and ready to start, let's do it.

The search

Believe it or not, just about everything about you will come into play in your search for scholarships — your ancestry, religion, place of birth, residence, parent's union or corporate affiliation, or simply your interest in a particular field can all be eligibility factors.

You and your child want to begin by selecting scholarship sources. Sit down with whatever research materials you have collected — scholarship directories; search service printouts; information from your union or company's endowments, if any; and other contact information you have discovered through various channels, such as the chamber of commerce or other sources. Select 20 to 30 different private sector scholarship sources. Next, you want to write to each source and ask for its scholarship application and specific requirements. The letter can be a general request-for-information form letter that can be photocopied (see page 36 for an example), but you should be specific about the name of the scholarship you are inquiring about on the envelope.

Write to each source as far in advance of its scholarship deadline as possible, and don't forget to send a self-addressed, stamped envelope—it not only expedites a reply, but some organizations won't respond without one.

Remember, on the outside of the envelope, list the name of the specific scholarship you are interested in so that the person opening the mail will know where to direct your inquiry. Addressing your envelope in this manner allows you to send a form letter to the scholarship sources.

Getting organized

As you receive information from each scholarship source, file it in the appropriate box to keep yourself organized. Then, when you have some quiet time after you have received some applications from the sources, read through each one carefully. You want to begin preparing to apply. Go through each box. Let's take a look at each now.

The government box

In the Government box, you will find that the state and federal forms are very similar, asking a multitude of questions regarding income, assets, and expenses. Don't automatically exclude yourself from state and federal funding

Sample request letter

Date

Scholarship Director
Scholarship Program Office
Address
City, State ZIP

Dear Scholarship Director:

Please send me application forms for the scholarships
or fellowships available to students. I have enclosed a
self-addressed, stamped envelope for your convenience in replying.

Sincerely,

Your name

Your name
(Street address)
(City, state, zip)

because you think that you or your family earn too much
money. These programs vary tremendously from state to
state, and the federal programs have changed quite a bit.
For example, there is no longer a $32,500 limit on the
amount parents can earn in order to qualify for a student
loan; however, because that limit has been raised to $45,000,

there will be less federal money to go around, so be sure to get in line early.

A bit of good news in the student loan arena is that the federal government no longer considers the value of your house or farm in determining the amount of aid for which you qualify. (See Part Two for more on government aid.)

The school endowments box

The School Endowments box should contain any information from scholarships awarded through the school. You will discover that sources in the School Endowments box are really just another form of private sector scholarships. The difference is that endowment money is given directly to the school and is administered exclusively by the school's financial aid office, so you must deal directly with the college. You'll find that the myths I talked about earlier also apply to these private endowments: Don't exclude yourself because of those old clichés regarding grades, financial status, deadlines, or age.

I will talk more about government aid in Part Two, but in order to understand how school endowments are awarded, it's important to talk about government funding a bit here. When you apply for government aid through the Free Application for Federal Student Aid (FAFSA), a report is sent to your school based on the information provided. The school uses this Student Aid Report (SAR) to determine how much money you are able to put towards your child's education. If it is less than your expected expenses, you have financial need and may receive university grants and other need-based awards.

Even if you don't think you qualify, you still want to fill out the FAFSA. Colleges now require this information to be on file, even for non-need-based endowments. As mentioned in Chapter 1, you will usually find a list of endowments

Federal Programs	Amount Awarded in Billions	
Generally available aid:		
Pell Grants	5.68	
Stafford Student Loans	14.12	
Supplemental Loans for Students	3.48	
Other	5.90	
Subtotal		29.18
Specially directed aid		2.24
Total Federal Aid		**31.42**

Source: The Chronicle of Higher Education, Almanac Issue (1 September 1995), p. 37. Figures are for academic year 1993-1994.

from alumni listed in the financial aid section of the college catalog. Often, endowments to schools are not advertised and may go unclaimed. For example, at a small school like USF, the total endowments average $20 million to $30 million per year. At Ivy League schools, endowments range from $100 million to $200 million-plus each year. Of those endowments, 10 to 15 percent goes to the financial aid office in the form of scholarships, fellowships, grants, and loans.

The private sector box

The material in your Private Sector box will all start to look the same once you have received one or two forms. Usually these forms are two pages long and ask where you are going to school, what you are going to major in, and why you think you deserve the scholarship. Some scholarship sources require that you join their organization. If the organization relates to your field of study, you should strongly consider joining because it will keep you informed (via newsletters, conferences, and more) about developments in that field.

Financial Aid Sources	Amount Awarded in Billions
Private Scholarships & Fellowships:	
Controlled & awarded by school	13.14
Public institutions	5.09
Private institutions	8.05

Source: National Center for Education Statistics. Figures are for the academic year 1995-1996.

Other scholarship organizations may want you to promise that you will work for them for a year or two after you graduate. The Dow Jones Newspaper Fund offers a scholarship for up to $20,000 for journalism, broadcasting, and communications students with the understanding that the student will intern with them for two years. This could even yield a permanent job for the student.

Private sector offerings

I have compiled just a sampling of some of the private sector scholarship sources. You will find thousands more in your search, but to give you an idea of what's out there, here are some examples.

For the 4ᵗʰ-12ᵗʰ grade student

Students in grades 4 through 12 can enter an essay competition and possibly receive an award to help with full to partial tuition to Space Camp. This competition was created by the **U.S. Space Camp Foundation**.

Phone: (800)63-SPACE
Web site: *www.spacecamp.com*

Private Scholarships & Fellowships	Amount Awarded in Billions
Controlled & awarded by the private sector	30.10

Source: Database Survey, National Scholarship Research Service, May 2000.

Students in grades 7 through 12 have the opportunity to win up to $5,000 from **Scholastic Inc**. All that is required is the ability to demonstrate a talent in art, photography, writing, or interdisciplines. Cash grants are awarded and can be used for any field of study.

Phone: (800)SCHOLASTIC
Web site: *www.scholastic.com*

The **Veterans of Foreign Wars of the United States** has an annual *Voice of Democracy Audio-Essay Scholarship Contest*. The contest is open to students in grades 10 through 12 who attend public, private, or parochial high schools. Awards range from $1,000 to $20,000.

Phone: (816)968-1117; Fax:(816)968-1157
Web site: *www.vfw.org*

For the undergraduate

"Average yet creative" is the punchline for junior telecommunications majors at Ball State University. **The David Letterman Telecommunications Scholarship Program** could pay your way to graduation if you are an average student with a very creative mind!

Phone: (317)285-1480
Web site: *www.bsu.edu/students/finaid/home.html*

Your tuition troubles could be gone with the wind! If you are a lineal descendant of a worthy Confederate soldier, contact the **United Daughters of the Confederacy** about its $400 to $1,500 scholarships.

Phone: (804)355-1636
Web site: *www.hsv.tis.nit/~maxs/UDC/index.html*

For women re-entry students, the **Jeanette Rankin Foundation** awards $1,000 to the winning woman aged 35 or older who is a U.S. citizen enrolled in a program of vocational-technical training or in an undergraduate program.

Written Inquiry: P.O. Box 6653, Athens, GA 30604

For the graduate

Think about the past, plan for the future! Princeton University's **Shelby Cullom Davis Center for Historical Studies** offers up to $55,000 per year in post-doctoral fellowships to highly recommended scholars who pursue research on an annual theme.

Phone: (609)258-4997

Minority graduate students who are studying in the fields of science and engineering qualify for **National Aeronautics and Space Administration Scholarships** if they are considering a career in space science and/or aerospace technology.

Phone: (202)453-8344

The **National Federation of the Blind** *(Hermione Grant Calhoun Scholarship)* offers $3,000 to legally blind women who are undergraduate or graduate students studying in any field.

Phone: (515)236-3366

For the international student

If you're an unmarried female under the age of 27 who promises not to wed until the completion of your next degree, you could be eligible for the *Alice Freeman Palmer Fellowship* of $4,000 for graduate studies in the United States or abroad.

Phone: (617)283-3525

Minority undergraduates with at least a 3.0 G.P.A. desiring to spend a semester or summer studying in a participating foreign university and who demonstrate leadership potential and extracurricular involvement in multicultural or international issues may qualify for *International Scholarships for Minorities* from the **American Institute for Foreign Studies**. There is one scholarship that consists of full program fees and transportation, and there are also five semester scholarships of $1,000.

Phone: (800)727-2437
Web site: *www.aifs.org*

AFS Intercultural Programs has created the *International Exchange Student Program* to give high school students financial assistance to study abroad for a semester or a year. Students live with host families and attend local secondary schools.

Phone: (800)AFS-INFO; Fax: (212)299-9090
Web site: *www.afs.org*

For all females

Are you a mature woman, head of your household, and looking to get ahead? The **Soroptimist International of the Americas** *Training Awards Program* will give you up to $3,000 plus an additional cash award of $10,000 for all fields of study.

Phone: (215)557-9300; Fax: (215)568-5200

Mervyn's California/Women's Sports Foundation Scholarship Fund offers $1,000 to college-bound high school senior girls involved in athletics. The program is not limited to California residents.

Phone: (800)227-3988; Fax: (516)542-4716
Web site: *www.lifetimetv.com/WoSport*

For female undergraduate students in the fields of science and social science, **The Association for Women in Science Educational Foundation** offers the *Dr. Vicki L. Schechtman Scholarship*. Award is for U.S. citizens with a minimum 3.0 G.P.A., and may be used for tuition, books, housing, research, equipment, etc.

Phone: (800)886-AWIS
Web site: *www.awis.org*

For all males

The **Phi Kappa Theta National Foundation Scholarship Program** offers undergraduate scholarships to members of the Phi Kappa Theta fraternity. Five scholarships are awarded based on financial need.

Phone: (317)872-9934

The **Young American Bowling Alliance** offers the *Chuck Hall Star of Tomorrow Scholarship* of $4,000 to male students who are amateur bowlers and members of the American Bowling Congress (ABC) or the Young American Bowling Alliance (YABA). Must be a high school senior or an undergraduate attending college, up to age 21 years of age.

Written Inquiry: 5301 S. 76th St., Greendale WI 53129

The **Maud Glover Folsom Foundation, Inc.** offers $2,500 to American males of Anglo-Saxon or German descent to age 35 for use in prep school, high school, college, and advanced education.

Written Inquiry: 10 North Road, Harwinton CT 06791

For all minorities

The **Jackie Robinson Foundation** offers scholarships of $5,000 per year for four years to college-bound minority high school seniors. The program includes counseling, as well as assistance in obtaining summer jobs and permanent employment after graduation.

Phone: (212)290-8600
Web site:
www.jackierobinson.org/Scholar/Prog/Src/lower.html

Ethnic minorities with disabilities, and ethnic minorities with disabilities who are gifted and talented meet the criteria for *Stanley E. Jackson Scholarship Awards* of $500 from the **Foundation for Exceptional Children**.

Phone: (703)264-3507
Web site: *www.cec.sped.org/fd/scholapp.htm*

Ethnic minority students enrolled at accredited colleges or universities who demonstrate financial need and academic excellence may qualify for $2,500 *Lena Chang Scholarship* awards from the **Nuclear Age Peace Foundation**. Requirements: two letters of recommendation, and an essay on ways to achieve peace in the Nuclear Age and how one hopes to contribute to that end.

Phone: (805)965-3443; Fax: (805)568-0466
Web site: *www.wagingpeace.org*

Religious

Scholarships are being offered by **The Heath Education Fund** to high school graduates who are from the southeastern United States and who wish to study ministry, missionary work, or social work.

Phone: (904)464-2877

The Memorial Foundation for Jewish Culture offers an *International Scholarship Program for Community Service,* which is open to any individual, regardless of country of origin, for undergraduate study that leads to careers in the Rabbinate, Jewish education, social work, or religious functionaries outside the United States, Israel, and Canada. Must commit to serve in a community of need for three years.

Phone: (212)679-4074

Various scholarships for students in the field of pastoral (religious) music are available from the **National Association of Pastoral Musicians**. Applying students must be a member of this organization in order to receive a scholarship.

Phone: (202)723-5800; Fax: (202)723-2262
Web site: *www.npm.org*

Corporate

How sweet it is! **Sara Lee Corporation** employees, their spouses, and their children can apply for a student loan of up to $2,500 for study at an accredited institution.

Phone: (312)726-2600

GTE offers scholarships to high school seniors who are dependents of full-time employees and who are planning to begin full-time study at an accredited undergraduate college or university.

Phone: (609)921-9000

Need a Midas touch in searching for scholarships? **The Midas International Corporation** offers scholarships to dependents of current Midas employees.

Phone: (312)565-7500

Students between the ages of 6 and 21 and who have moderate to profound hearing loss are being given the opportunity to win scholarships by the **Alexander Graham Bell Association for the Deaf**. In order to qualify, students must use speech and residual hearing and/or speech-reading as a primary form of communication.

Phone: (202)337-5220
Web site: *www.agbell.org*

Aviation

The **Vertical Flight Foundation** is awarding scholarships up to $2,000 to undergraduate and graduate students who have proven interests in pursuing careers in some aspect of helicopter or vertical flight.

Phone: (703)684-6777; Fax: (703)739-9279
Web site: *www.vtol.org*

The **EAA Aviation Foundation** offers two *Aviation Achievement Scholarships* of $500 and more annually to individuals who are active in sport aviation. The scholarships are to be used in order to further the recipient's aviation education training.

Phone: (888)EAA-EAA9

Web site: *www.eaa.org*

Scholarships are being made available for students studying in the fields of aviation and aerospace by the **Ninety-Nines, Inc. International**. Eligibility requirements vary.

Phone: (405)685-7969; Fax: (405)685-7985

For woman flyers who prefer helicopters, **International Women Helicopter Pilots/Whirly Girls** scholarships grant $4,000 to encourage careers in vertical flight.

Phone: (602)263-0190; Fax: (602)264-5812

Unusual

High school seniors and undergraduates with the surname of Gatlin or Gatling might want to take a shot at the **John Gatling** (Inventor of the Gatling Gun) **Scholarship Program** which offers full scholarships up to $7,000 at North Carolina State University.

Phone: (919)515-3671; Fax: (919)515-6021

Investigating scholarship possibilities? **The Association of Former Agents of the US Secret Service (AFAUSS)** offers the *J. Clifford Dietrich and Julie Y. Cross Scholarships* of $500 to $2,500 to undergraduate law enforcement or police administration students. You do have to give your real name, but fingerprints won't be necessary.

Written Inquiry: P.O. Box 848, Annandale, VA 22003-0848

Celebrity

The proof is in the pudding! **Bill Cosby** and his wife, Camille, have been acclaimed as 'The First Family of Philanthropy' for their generous donations to various colleges in excess of $28 million dollars.

This is certainly one house with high equity! Morehouse College received $1 million from **Oprah Winfrey** to establish the *Oprah Winfrey Endowed Scholarship Fund.*

Phone: (800)851-1254; Fax: (404)524-5635

The essay

Most organizations awarding scholarships require an essay as part of the application process. The essay is the most important part of the private sector scholarship application. It should describe who you are and what you want to be. But don't make it paragraph after paragraph about activities and achievements—be creative! After all, who wants to read: "My name is..., my school is..., my activities are...," for hundreds or thousands of students? You want to be memorable.

A common misconception is that the bigger the words and the more complicated the sentences, the more impressive you sound. The key to a good essay, however, is to write plainly, using a style based on strong verbs and bold, direct expressions of action. The beginning and ending sentences of each paragraph should be especially strong. Vary the rhythm of sentences, balancing long against short, fast against slow, and general against specific. Don't use clichés, and don't overly use a word—you want the reader to pay attention to the content of your essay, not the words themselves.

As you write, keep in mind the theme of your essay and don't stray from that central idea. Each paragraph should flow well into the next, carrying on the common theme or idea. The introduction should obviously introduce this idea, and the conclusion should summarize it. The rest of the essay is built around this theme.

The following excerpt from the University of California at Los Angeles' (UCLA) application material emphasizes the importance of the essay and contains good advice no matter what scholarship you are applying for or where you are going to college:

> *The essay is an important part of your application for admission and for scholarships.*
>
> *For these purposes, the University seeks information that will distinguish you from other applicants. You may wish, therefore, to write about your experiences, achievements, and goals. You might, for example, discuss an important life experience and what you learned from it. You might also describe unusual circumstances, challenges, or hardships you have faced. School activities and experiences are also topics to discuss in your essay but they do not need to be the focus.*
>
> *Rather than listing activities, describe your level of achievement in areas you have pursued — including employment or volunteer activities — and the personal qualities revealed by the time and effort you have devoted to them.*
>
> *Also, discuss your interest in your intended field of study. If you have a disability, you may also include a description of its impact on your experiences, goals, and aspirations.*
>
> *The University seeks information about any exceptional achievements such as activities, honors, awards, employment, or volunteer work that demonstrates your motivation, achievement, leadership, and commitment.*

Just as important as what you write is how your essay looks—first impressions are important! Make sure your essay is neatly typed, well-written, and does not contain grammatical errors or misspelled words. Careless errors and sloppiness send the message that you don't care, and if you don't care, why should the reader? Take the time to carefully proofread your essay, use the spellchecker in your word processing program, and make sure to use a reader-friendly font, such as 12-point Times New Roman. The margins should be one inch, writing double-spaced, and the first line of each new paragraph indented a half-inch on the left. If you are using a typewriter, there should be two spaces between each sentence; if you're using a computer, there should be only one. Don't forget to add a title. It should reflect the topic of your essay, and shouldn't be italicized or put in quotation marks. Print your essay on 8 ½ x 11 white-bond paper, and staple the pages together in the upper left-hand corner.

Now that you know the basics of essay writing, you may be trying to decide what to write. If you are struggling to make a decision on a topic, start putting down ideas on scratch paper: Why do you want to go to college? Why do you want to major in your chosen subject? Is there a specific incident that inspired you to pursue your goal? If you're involved in extracurricular activities, is there a certain event or day that stands out to you? What experiences have helped shape your life or have influenced you?

Take these thoughts and just start writing—you can fine-tune it later. If a lot of thought goes into what you're writing, it will show.

Put together a curriculum vitae

Along with the essay, students should include a curriculum vitae (resume). This is the place to list your activities and achievements, and it will help the reader to know more about you.

Sample Curriculum Vitae

Awards and Scores

National Merit Semifinalist

4.0 GPA (9–11) (no grades yet for 12)

Rank in Class: 1

SAT Scores: 750 Math, 720 Verbal

Achievement Test Scores: 770 Eng., 720 Math II, 680 Bio.

AP Test Scores: 5 English Language, 3 Calculus BC,
   3 Biology, 3 U.S. History

Advanced Placement Scholar with Honor (1992)

High Honors in Golden State Exam for Algebra (1988)
   and for Geometry (1989)

Honors in Golden State Exam for Chemistry (1991)

LHS Award for Academic Excellence (Fall/Spring 1990),
   (Fall/Spring 1991)

Sandia Women's Committee Math/Science Award
   recipient (May 1992)

Activities

School: California Scholarship Federation (CSF) (9–12)

   Tutoring: (Committee head and member) Volunteer,
      all subjects

   Fund raising: (Committee member) Sales, after school
      and at downtown Livermore functions

Sacramento Trip: (Committee head) Arranged CSF trip to
Capitol to protest state budget cuts in education; 150 CSF
members from seven high schools attended. Arranged for press
coverage; had representatives from the Governor's office,
Superintendent Honig's office, and Speaker Will Brown's office.
Reserved main hearing room of the Capitol for this event and
served as moderator.

   Math Club (11)

   Academic Olympics (10, 12)

   International Pen-Pal (Spain) (11-12)

Activities (cont.)

Community: Cross-age tutoring for local middle school—all
 subjects, grades 6 through 8
 Same-age tutoring—individual, Spanish and math

Sports

 High School JV Tennis Team (10)

Work Experience

 Snack bar worker at horse boarding and training
  stables (1988-1991)
 Clerical services at doctor's office (1990)
 Summer student at Sandia National Laboratories in
  Livermore (through Associated Western
  Universities); did research on air pollution and
  other environmental issues; performed
  chemistry and physics research (1992)
 Rehired part-time for school year at Sandia National
  Laboratories (1992-1993)

Hobbies

 Needlework: cross-stitch, embroidery, needlepoint,
  making formal dresses
 Piano lessons: 12 years and continuing
 Spanish: speaking and literature

The scholarship application

When filling out scholarship application forms, be complete, concise, and creative. People who read these applications want to know the real you, not just your name. Those reading the applications may be special committees comprised of experts in their fields, education professionals, or the executive director of the organization or scholarship sponsor. Scholarship applications should clearly emphasize your ambitions, motivations, and what makes you different from everyone else. Be original!

Like your essay, the application should be typewritten and neat. I had a complaint from one foundation about a student who had an excellent background and qualifications but used a crayon to fill out the application. Others use hard-to-read pencils or various colors of pen to fill it out. Still others write so small you can barely read it, while others use sprawling cursive that is hard to interpret. Some students leave important questions blank, and others even spell their chosen major wrong! Mistakes like these are unprofessional and show the awarding foundation that you didn't put much effort into it. If you don't take the proper time and thought in filling out your application, what kind of effort will you put into your schoolwork? Nobody is going to want to sponsor a student who doesn't respect the foundation enough to properly fill out its application.

Once the application is filled out, photocopy it and create a master file for copies of the application, essay, and other supporting documents. Attach your essay to each application. If requested, also include: a curriculum vitae, extracurricular activities sheet (usually one page), transcripts, SAT or ACT scores, letters of recommendation (usually one each from a teacher, employer, and friend, outlining your moral character), any newspaper articles about you, copies of awards/certificates received, and a copy of the letter of acceptance to your college/university (if you've already applied). You may wish to organize this information in a clear plastic report folder, putting your name, school name, and grade level.

You might also include your photograph, whether it's a high school picture or a snapshot of you working at your favorite hobby. This helps the selection committee feel a little closer to you. Instead of just seeing a name, they will have a face to match it.

Mail your applications in early, at least a month before the deadline.

You should keep copies of what you send to each of the scholarship sources and keep each application in its own file. On the outside of the file, you might rate your chances of getting the scholarship on a scale of 1 to 10.

Application checklist

The following supporting documents may be requested with your application. I suggest you make a master file for these documents and photocopy them. Then you can just pull a copy from your file and attach it to the application upon request.

Application Checklist

- ❑ Your essay.
- ❑ Extracurricular activities sheet.
- ❑ Curriculum vitae.
- ❑ Transcripts.
- ❑ SAT or ACT scores.
- ❑ Letters of recommendation.
- ❑ Any personally related newspaper articles or material.

The calendar

I find it helpful to keep a calendar with deadlines circled so you can stay organized. You can hang it above your three scholarship boxes so it is easily visible.

If a scholarship application deadline has passed, save the application package for the next year. If you are turned down for a scholarship, don't worry; some organizations want to see if you will apply a second time. The important point is to stay motivated and be persistent.

Chapter 3

Some Final Words on Private Sector Aid

S o there you have a simple way to prepare, organize, and apply. Keep in mind that scholarships are not only rewarding monetarily, but are very prestigious as well. They look fantastic on your resume and, most likely, will be recognized immediately by your colleagues, professors, and future employers.

You can receive more than one scholarship, and many are usually renewable for up to four years. It is important that you understand the criteria upon which your scholarship is given. If you must return annually to the financial aid office to sign for your scholarship, then be sure that you are there at the correct time. I remember a friend of mine who had a *full* scholarship at USF. All he had to do was go to the financial aid office each year and sign for it. One year, he forgot to do that, and they gave his scholarship to someone else. Needless to say, he was very disappointed. Instead of enjoying free time that year, he had to work at San Francisco's Fisherman's Wharf to make ends meet.

Most private sector scholarships are given directly to you to spend on tuition, room and board, books, or parking fees.

The rules in the private sector are simple: In order to apply, you must 1) attend an accredited institution, whether it is a two-year, four-year, or a vocational school and 2) take at least two classes, or six units, per semester/quarter/year, allowing even part-time students to qualify.

There's something for everyone, in every situation. Check out every option and apply. It's really that easy.

Part II

Government Aid

Chapter 4

Applying for Federal Financial Aid

Fully 68 percent of all full-time undergraduate students in the United States receive some form of financial assistance. The aid comes from two primary sources: the federal government and the schools these students attend. The majority of assistance is in the form of grants and loans, with employment bringing up the rear.

As discussed in the previous section, all students who wish to apply for federal financial assistance need to complete the Free Application for Federal Student Aid (FAFSA). For last-minute filers, I strongly recommend using FAFSA on the Internet to file your application. It's faster than the paper application and offers an automatic calculation of your Expected Family Contribution once you have completed the form. The Web address to file online is *www.fafsa.ed.gov*.

If you filed a paper application last year, you will soon receive a Renewal

FAFSA. The Renewal FAFSA has much of your information pre-printed on the form. You can file this via mail or Internet. To access your Renewal FAFSA online, you will need an Electronic Access Code (EAC).

If you filed electronically last year, use the EAC you were provided then. Your EAC will not change from year to year. If you did not, your EAC should be mailed to you. If you just plain can't find it, go to the FAFSA on the Web site and request your EAC and the Department of Education will mail it to you.

Believe it or not, completing the FAFSA is relatively straightforward. The most common mistake most people make when completing the FAFSA is failing to read the instructions. Most of the information you need to supply on the form is either known to you or is at your fingertips. Be prepared to spend about an hour to complete the application.

In order to get started, you will need the following:

- ☉ Your Social Security card and driver's license.
- ☉ W-2 forms or other records of income earned.
- ☉ Your (and your spouse's, if you are married) Federal Income Tax Return.
- ☉ Your parent's Federal Income Tax Return.
- ☉ Records of other untaxed income received, such as welfare benefits, social security benefits, TANF, veteran's benefits, or military or clergy allowances.
- ☉ Current bank statements and records of stocks, bonds, and other investments.
- ☉ Business or farm records, if applicable.
- ☉ Your alien registration card (if you are not a U.S. citizen).

Once you file your FAFSA, the Central Processing Service for the Department of Education receives and processes your data. It applies a number of edits to determine your eligibility for federal aid programs. It also applies a formula known as Federal Methodology to the data you provide to determine an Expected Family Contribution. After your data is processed by CPS, it is transmitted electronically to the colleges you indicated should receive it. The colleges, in turn, interpret that data and decide whether or not they are able to make an award. If they can't, they will contact you either by phone or by mail to request further information. Once everything is set, the financial aid administrator who reviews your material will determine your eligibility for financial aid based on need.

Need

The data you supply on the FAFSA is used by financial aid offices to determine your need for financial aid. There are a few components that determine how much aid you can receive.

First, you file the FAFSA. The Department of Education puts your data through a formula known as Federal Methodology to calculate an Expected Family Contribution (EFC). The EFC basically tells how much of your resources are available after allowances for living, taxes, and savings, to contribute toward education based on your state of residence, household size, number in college, and student and parent income and asset information.

Next, the school you attend establishes a Cost of Attendance (COA). The COA is composed of tuition, room and board, fees, and estimated expenses (books, supplies, and personal).

The Expected Family Contribution and Cost of Attendance are used to determine your financial need. Financial need is calculated by subtracting the EFC from the COA and is a guideline in determining how much need-based financial aid you may receive.

The financial aid office then uses the need-based resources it has available to try and meet your financial need. Here is an example to demonstrate:

Sally files her FAFSA and a few weeks later receives her Student Aid Report (SAR). She notes that the EFC on the SAR is "01200" or $1,200. Her school has a COA of $18,000. So, using the formula above we find that Sally's need is $16,800.

The financial aid office then uses this information to construct a financial aid package. For example, the college offers the following:

Institutional Grant	$5,000
Federal Pell Grant	$1,550
Federal SEOG	$1,000
Federal Subsidized Stafford Loan	$3,500
Federal Perkins Loan	$1,000
Federal Work Study	$1,600
Total aid:	$13,650

What this tells us is that if Sally's need for financial aid is $16,800, the financial aid office was only able to meet $13,650 of that. The difference between the two is called unmet need. In this case, Sally's unmet financial need is $3,250. What that means to Sally is that she will have to contribute more than her EFC in order to meet her educational costs. Unmet need is a common occurrence in financial aid packages. The school is under no obligation to meet your need for financial aid, and in many cases, is simply unable to do so given the types and amounts of funding at their disposal. What the financial aid office does, to the best of its ability, is to meet as much of your need with the resources it has available. Those resources may include scholarships, grants, loans, and work.

Types of federal assistance

Federal Pell Grants

Pell Grants are available to the neediest of undergraduate students only. Pell Grants are gift aid and, as such, do not have to be repaid.

Federal Stafford Loans

The Stafford Loan comes in two flavors: Federal Family Education Loan Program (FFELP) and William D. Ford Direct Loans. What's the difference? FFELP loans are Stafford Loans that are borrowed through banks and guaranteed by the states or their designated guarantee agency. Direct Loans are Stafford Loans that are made by the school and funded/ guaranteed "directly" through the federal government. Your school can tell you in which program they participate. Regardless, they are one and the same. A Stafford Loan is a Stafford Loan. Freshmen can borrow up to $2,625, sophomores up to $3,500, juniors/seniors up to $5,500, and graduate students up to $18,500.

Stafford Loans can be subsidized, unsubsidized, or a combination of both. Students receiving subsidized Stafford Loans pay no interest on the loan while they are attending college on at least a part-time basis. While a student is in school and during the six-month grace period, the federal government pays the interest for you. Borrowers of unsubsidized Stafford Loans are responsible for the interest during the in-school and grace periods. You can either pay the interest on a quarterly basis or allow the interest to accrue. If you choose to allow the interest to accrue, the interest will be added to the principal and will compound over time. In effect, interest will be paid on interest and principal and so forth.

You cannot borrow more than your cost of attendance minus any other financial aid. The Stafford Loan (be it a FFELP or Direct Loan) is a variable interest rate loan that has a cap on the interest rate of 8.25 percent. The interest rate changes annually and is calculated by taking the bond equivalent rate of the last auction of the 91-day Treasury Bill and adding 2.7 percent. The interest rate charged on Stafford Loans changes every July 1st. Repayment begins on these loans six months after you no longer are attending school on at least a part-time basis. The six months before repayment is called the grace period.

If you have never borrowed a Stafford Loan, you will receive detailed information regarding your Stafford Loan from the financial aid office and when you attend your entrance interview. The entrance interview is a mandatory one-time session where the school will explain to you your rights and responsibilities relevant to your loans.

If you borrow through the FFELP program, you will have to choose a lender. The vast majority of banking institutions participate in the program, so you may even be able to use the bank you have your other accounts through as your lender. However, many schools prefer you borrow through lenders they have established working relationships with and may also suggest you use the guarantee agency used by the state in which they are located.

Federal PLUS Loans

Federal Parent Loans for Undergraduate Students (PLUS) are borrowed in the name of the *parent*. The interest rate varies, but is capped at 9 percent. PLUS Loans are made either through the school (Direct Loans) or through a private lender (FFELP Loans). If you are independent or if you are denied a PLUS loan based on adverse credit reporting, you may ask the financial aid office to consider you for additional

Unsubsidized Stafford Loan eligibility—up to $4,000 for freshmen or sophomores and $5,000 for juniors or seniors. You will need to write a letter to the financial aid office, request Unsubsidized consideration, and enclose a copy of the denial letter you received from the lender.

Campus-Based Programs

Campus-based funds are awarded by the school. Each year the Department of Education makes an allocation of funds to each school for these programs. It is up to the school to determine your eligibility for and award these funds.

Supplemental Education Opportunity Grant (SEOG)

SEOG is a grant available for very needy undergraduates only. Awards range from $100 to $4,000.

Federal Work Study (FWS)

FWS provides jobs to undergraduate and graduate students who are then paid on an hourly rate, at minimum wage or above.

Perkins Loans

The Perkins Loan carries a 5 percent fixed-interest rate; repayment doesn't begin until nine months after the student graduates or drops below half-time attendance (six credit hours). The maximum annual loan amount is $3,000 for undergraduate students and $5,000 for graduate students. The standard repayment term is 120 months.

Many schools give Perkins Loans for the first two years of study to augment your ability to borrow. This is because the maximum Stafford Loan a student can take as a freshman is $2,625 and, as a sophomore, $3,500. Perkins funding can be renewed through the junior and senior years of study (in fact some graduate students may receive Perkins Loans), but because of the limited availability of funding for this program, it is not likely for a student to receive it after the sophomore year.

Deadlines

When it comes to filing applications, there are some deadlines to keep in mind.

- ⊕ The CSS Profile Application can usually be filed as early as October 15. Be sure to read your admissions material carefully to determine whether or not you need to complete the application and when you need to file it by.

- ⊕ February 1 is the typical priority filing deadline for the FAFSA for incoming students.

- ⊕ March 1 is most often the priority filing deadline for continuing students.

Pay close attention to filing deadlines. Filing on time ensures that you receive maximum consideration for all the types of aid that are available.

Chapter 5

Applying for Institutional Aid

Although federal aid programs are funded in the billions of dollars, those dollars are distributed to many students. Thus, federal aid alone is often unable to help meet your financial need. The good news is, private colleges offer many grant, loan, and work programs to help make access to their institutions affordable. Many of these colleges offer non-need-based scholarship assistance, such as the school endowments discussed in the previous section. Consideration for some scholarship aid is usually determined by reviewing your application for admission. Factors used to determine your eligibility are numerous. They can include: high school G.P.A., rank in class, SAT/ACT scores, the program you are applying for, and even your geographical location. How do you know what you qualify for?

The admissions office of the college to which you apply is normally responsible for determining your eligibility for scholarship assistance. You will be notified whether you have received an award in your acceptance letter.

However, assistance from the college does not end with the admissions process. There are two basic ways that colleges determine your eligibility for need-based institutional assistance. The first is the FAFSA and the second is the CSS Profile Application. You may not be required to file the CSS Profile. Your college will tell you whether or not you are required to submit the Profile application in the admissions packet you receive.

If you are required to file the Profile, you can do so online. The Web address at which you can complete the Profile is *www.collegeboard.org*. Click on the Profile icon for instructions.

Colleges use the Profile application for two reasons. First, the Profile application asks more detailed questions about your family's finances. Thus, the college is better able to determine your eligibility for institutional assistance. Institutional aid is, in many cases, very limited. By collecting more information up front about your finances, the school can best decide how to apply its resources. Second, many schools are under a great deal of pressure to notify you of your eligibility for financial aid very early. Their research shows that there is a greater chance that you will enroll if they get to you first. The only way to do that is to have a reliable estimation of your federal Expected Family Contribution (EFC). The CSS Profile uses the data you provide to estimate your EFC. The college uses that estimate, along with the additional data it collects through the Profile, to estimate your eligibility for federal financial aid and to determine what, if any, institutional assistance they can provide.

Types of institutional assistance

Institutional assistance comes in the same form as federal financial assistance, but may also include non-need-based scholarship assistance. Most private colleges and some public schools have the ability to offer need-based grants or work-study opportunities. Some even offer their own institutional loan program. The schools employ a number of methods to determine your eligibility for their programs, but generally tend to follow the federal guidelines in determining your need. Availability of funding directly from colleges varies by school. Some schools are able to offer more assistance because of larger endowments or simply discount the tuition more significantly than their competitors. In the end, the amount and types of institutional assistance will vary widely among schools.

Scholarships

Many schools offer scholarships to qualified applicants. Bear in mind that such scholarships are highly competitive. Depending on how competitive the school and the program to which you are applying are, you may not even qualify despite being a top-notch student in all other respects.

Grants

Need-based grants are widely available at private colleges and universities. In most cases, an offer of an institutional need-based grant is nothing more than a discount on tuition. Colleges look at their overall costs and determine, on average, how much they need to receive in real dollars from each student in order to operate. That number is called net tuition revenue—the amount of money the college receives directly after institutional assistance is factored out.

Work study

Some colleges offer all of their students opportunities to work regardless of whether they are eligible for Federal

Work Study. In some cases, these schools will employ students whether or not they qualify for need-based assistance. Check with your school to find out if it can offer employment to you.

Loans

Beyond federal loan programs, many schools offer their own institutional loan programs. Normally, the college will inform you on your award letter if you are eligible for a college-administered loan.

Chapter 6

The Financial Aid Package

n the financial aid administrator's bag of tricks are a number of sources of assistance he or she can give to eligible students. That aid might include federal, state, or institutional (money directly from the college) sources. The administrator will put together a "package" based on many factors. When will you find out what you are receiving for the upcoming year?

If you are an incoming student, you will find out shortly after you receive your acceptance letter from the admissions office. If you are a returning or continuing student, you should find out sometime between May and July (results will vary depending upon how well your school has its act together and whether or not you filed on time).

Well, you've applied for aid and received your financial aid package. What's next? That all depends. If you are an incoming student, you will probably have to supply the financial aid office with your tax return should you decide to enroll. But first and foremost, you should start to compare the different offers you receive. You'll need to get out a pad and pencil and sit down at the table and compare schools not only on how much your actual cost will be, but also on academic merits. In that sense, you may choose a more expensive school based on the fact that it offers the exact program you are interested in rather than a close match. Finally, it's not always the least expensive school that is the best choice. Many times, you do get what you pay for. Keep that in mind as you review.

If you are a continuing student, you should look to see if there have been any significant changes to the amount of aid you receive. If there has been a sizable change, you need to ask yourself what has changed in your family's financial situation that could have caused the change in assistance. Some likely factors can include pay increases, selling off of assets (stocks, bonds, etc.), having one less family member in college, rolling over your IRA to a Roth IRA, and a host of other factors. You may also need to supply the financial aid office with additional information (that is, tax returns, W-2 statements, verification worksheet, etc.) should they request it. If you receive mail from the financial aid office, open it promptly and read it thoroughly.

Examining the financial aid package

Once you have received your financial aid package, your work can truly begin. In the case of continuing students, that can mean no more than comparing last year's award to this year's. For incoming students, the task is a little more involved. You will need to gather together all of the offers you have received and compare them to evaluate who has made the best offer of assistance.

Comparing financial aid offers is as easy as adding and subtracting. Two issues need to be addressed. First, how much will it cost? That can be answered by looking at the Cost of Attendance (COA) breakdown on the award letter (if there isn't one or if it is not broken down, call the financial aid administrator and ask him or her to break it down for you, category by category). You are looking for specific costs of tuition, room and board (if you will be living on campus), and any additional fees. Add these numbers together. Now subtract from that the advance deposit you will have to pay to confirm your attendance. The result is the amount that it will cost to attend the particular school you are looking at for one academic year (roughly September through May).

Next, review the financial aid offer. As we've discussed, there are basically three types of aid: grants, loans, and work. First, determine how much you have received in grant assistance. Then examine the assistance through loans.

Here's where it can get tricky. Look for a Stafford Loan and perhaps a Perkins Loan. If there are others, *do not* include them immediately. Now, add your grants and loans together. Finally, subtract your grants and loans from your cost. The result is what you will have to pay to attend that particular school.

Go ahead and do this with all of your other offers and compare your cost for each school. Start eliminating.

Some other things to consider. When you calculated the cost for each school, you only included the Stafford and Perkins Loans listed in your award. This puts each school on a level playing field. Some schools may offer a loan of their own or a PLUS Loan on the award letter itself. You have to be cautious when this happens.

If you plan on applying for a PLUS or other loan already, then don't sweat it. Just include the amount of loan you can afford in your other offers to keep it fair and to give you the best guide to your expenses. If you don't plan on borrowing at all, simply do not include loans.

What about work study? Many offers you receive will include work, be it Federal Work Study (FWS) or other campus employment award. Don't include this in your calculations. A student who receives a work offer will actually have to earn that award by finding a job on campus. Work in an aid offer is not a guarantee of employment. It is also not mandatory that the student accept such an award. Work is an opportunity, not an obligation.

There you have it: how to compare aid offers in a nutshell. Well, almost. Remember, college is an investment and a mighty expensive one at that. This is serious business. You have to be happy with the college you choose for four or more years. You have to be confident that the school does, in fact, offer the course of study you want to pursue. So, after you consider the financial aspects of your decision, remember to take into account academic and personal factors in order to make an informed choice.

Getting the best deal possible

Let's face it: The financial aid process is confusing and complicated. The first step to ensuring that you are getting the best deal possible is to educate yourself about how the process works.

So, how do you know if the school has done all it can for you? The answer is simple: You have to *ask*. Now, how you go about asking is another matter altogether, but one that warrants some discussion. Here's my suggested approach.

One of the most important relationships you can establish is the one with your financial aid advisor. Always call him or her when you have questions. In the end, the advisor has the final say in how much assistance you can receive. He or she is also the most knowledgeable and best prepared person to go to when it comes to finding assistance when there appears to be no hope left. Keep the financial aid office and your financial aid advisor foremost in your thoughts when it comes to paying for your education.

Look at the financial aid award. Can you afford the estimated cost to attend this school? If yes, you're still not off the hook. See if your need has been met. If it hasn't, then you have a right to complain. Well, maybe not complain. But, you should at the very minimum make contact with the financial aid advisor to see why the school was not able to meet your financial need. This is especially important if you simply cannot afford the college of your choice given your current circumstances and ability to pay. Sometimes, you will get a response like, "We have offered the most financial aid possible, given our available funds and your need for financial aid." That's great, but that isn't the end of it. Tell the financial aid administrator what you *can* afford. Ask if there is anything he or she can do to come closer to what you truly are able to pay. Sure, you can lowball a figure for them, but it won't work. If they're close, see if they can get a little closer.

Some schools will negotiate a better offer with you. This is especially true if they are close to getting you to enroll. Others will not negotiate, plain and simple. But you'll never know unless you ask.

I've said this before and it deserves repeating here: Be nice. That's right! I know you want to be a strong advocate for yourself or your student, but being argumentative or abusive to those who would help you is *very* counterproductive. Remember, ultimately, this is a business arrangement. Sometimes considerations can be made, sometimes not. What's most important is that you asked. That will *definitely* not hurt!

Good financial aid administrators will actually help you through this task, as it is something they deal with daily. They'll ask most of the questions and guide you through the process. There is no shame in doing this. After all, you're only looking out for your best interests.

Impact of outside scholarships

Okay, you've done your homework, researched available sources of scholarships through various scholarship directories, the free scholarship search services available on the Internet, and you applied to every scholarship for which you are eligible.

What happens next? With any luck, you win a scholarship. Unfortunately, that's not all there is to it.

You'll need to report your outside scholarship to the financial aid office at your college. In some cases there will be no consequence to you by doing this; in others, your financial aid may be affected.

Basically, there are three different approaches that your school might take when viewing your outside scholarship:

☉ **Approach One:** The school will first *meet* your unmet financial need. Next, they will reduce or replace your self-help component(s) (self-help basically means work-study or loans). Finally, once your need has been met and your self-help has been reduced or eliminated, any remaining scholarship funds will reduce need-based grant assistance dollar for dollar or will be applied in part to further reduce loan/work and in part against a need-based grant. However, it will *not* affect merit (or non-need-based) scholarships, Pell, VA benefits, or, in most cases, state grants.

- **Approach Two:** The school will meet any unmet need, then reduce your need-based grant assistance dollar for dollar.
- **Approach Three:** The school will reduce your need-based grant assistance dollar for dollar regardless of your unmet financial need. Very mean, not to mention unpopular.

As you can see, Approach One is the fairest application of policy, while Approach Three is just plain greedy.

So, what if your school's policy employs Approach Three? Well, to serve your best interests, know how the school determines your eligibility for need-based assistance. Know what your unmet financial need is, then talk to the financial aid administrator. Ask why you cannot use your scholarship to meet your unmet financial need. You probably won't get a break from schools that use Approaches One or Two, but I'd be willing to bet you might have some luck with a school that uses Approach Three.

Fortunately, most schools use an approach like numbers one or two. So, if you're lucky, you will be able to take advantage of any outside resource you might receive.

Doing your part

We've talked a lot about the do's and don'ts and the technical aspects that help make the financial aid process a bit smoother. But we haven't talked about your responsibilities.

Yes, you do have responsibilities when it comes to financial aid and your financial aid package. The financial aid office assumes you understand the part you must play in order to receive your aid. What I've discovered, however, is that this part is not always clearly defined. With that in mind, here are some tips:

1. **Requests for information.** When the financial aid office sends a letter, they actually expect that you'll read it and respond to it if needed. If your student is away at school, open his or her mail from the financial aid office. Trust me, this will save you lots of headaches later. If there is a request for information, you'll be able to take the appropriate action needed to satisfy that request.

2. **If you don't understand something.** So, you received a request for information, but you are not sure exactly what the financial aid office wants. What to do? Call them. Believe it or not, aid administrators expect that you will call when they send out large mailings. They want to answer your questions and make sure that you not only understand why something is needed, but also to ensure that you send the correct information the first time.

3. **Stafford Loans.** If your financial aid package contains a Stafford Loan, the financial aid office expects that you will follow up whenever necessary. When you sign a promissory note, they expect you to be worried when your loan hasn't been paid to your account. So, if you receive a bill late in the semester that shows that your loan has not yet been paid, it's time to call your lender. If you are at a school that is a direct lender, call the school's financial aid office to make sure there isn't a problem. If your loan doesn't get paid by the last day of classes, you may lose your loan entirely! Stay on top of this process. Of course, the financial aid office does follow up on loans for which it has not received payment, but don't take a chance on falling through the cracks!

The financial aid process is a two-way street. It can get complicated and confusing sometimes, but by remembering to do your part and by working with the financial aid office, you'll have a lot less to worry about!

Work-study programs

Most schools offer work-study programs as part of the financial aid package. This offer is *not* an obligation, but an opportunity. Sure, if you're a freshman you might end up having to work in the dining halls slinging grease, but, hey, it's only a couple hours a week. If you are a continuing or currently enrolled student, it will soon be time to start hunting or making sure you have a job secured for the upcoming semester. Typically, April is the month to find a job.

Take advantage of this opportunity. Some campus jobs are trivial (office assistant) and some are not (student manager). You'd be amazed at the range of jobs available on campus.

You also might be surprised to find out just how much a campus job can help. I worked 20 hours a week as an undergraduate and managed to actually reduce the amount of Stafford Loan I had to borrow. I estimate I saved nearly $7,000 in loan indebtedness by working.

I'll bet you also might be surprised to find out that statistics show that students who work (or generally participate in activities on campus) tend to get *better* grades than those who do not. Part of your college education includes extracurricular activities. Working is just one of the many ways you can broaden your college experience. Get involved!

If your financial aid award contains an offer of Federal Work Study, you can also pursue a community service position *off* campus. Furthermore, community service looks great on a resume. Ask someone in your financial aid office or student employment office about opportunities in the community.

A word about an offer to work: Many families assume that work-study or campus employment is deductible from the student bill. This is not the case. It is money that is set aside to pay the student's wages as he or she works on campus. If you're receiving an award letter for the first time (you're an incoming student, for example), look carefully at your awards and the cost of attendance outlined in your award letter. Charges you'll actually incur from the college include tuition, fees, and room and board. Items that aren't charged directly to you, but expenses that you'll have nonetheless include books, personal expenses, loan fees, and transportation. If you are unsure about what your actual charges are or may be, phone the college's bursar (billing) office and ask.

When you are trying to figure out how much it will cost to attend, add the costs that you will actually be charged (tuition, fees, room/board) and subtract financial aid (grants, loans) to get an estimate of your out-of-pocket costs. As I said, don't include work.

Finally, if your financial aid package does not include work, be sure to ask the financial aid or student employment office if there is any way work can be added to your package. Many schools are able to offer campus employment to students who do not qualify for need-based assistance.

The eleventh hour

There has been a lot of banter in the media about negotiating your financial aid offer. I thought I'd share my thoughts on this topic with you here.

If you are planning on attending a private college this fall, you might want to give the financial aid office a call and see if you have received the most financial aid that they can offer.

I never thought I'd encourage this practice, but the fact of the matter is, colleges *are* flexible when it comes to offers of financial assistance. Those who ask for more assistance are receiving it. It is a fact.

Many of you have made your college decision and are getting ready to send in your advance deposit and enroll-ment confirmation. Call the financial aid office first. If they are aware that you have paid your deposit, they are less likely to offer you additional funding or, at most, will offer less additional funding had you not paid your deposit. Of course, the reason for this is plain: If you have already paid, you are very likely to be enrolling.

If you do not have unusual circumstances, offer to share financial aid award letters of their competitors who have offered you more assistance. Use other offers for leverage. If one school has provided more assistance, ask if your school of choice can match or simply come closer to meeting the offer of support given by its competitor.

Outside of buying a home, college is the single largest expense you will have in your lifetime. It is imperative that you ensure you are getting the best deal possible at your first-choice institution.

How should you approach asking? Here's my tip list:

- ⊕ Have the student make the phone call.
- ⊕ Thank them for their already generous offer.
- ⊕ Ask (politely) if they can do anything to im-prove the offer.
- ⊕ Provide any documentation they may ask for, including copies of other colleges' award letters.

- If asked how much you can afford, be honest and reasonable. You don't have anything to lose by telling the truth about how much you think you can pay. At worst, you will still have the original offer.

- Follow up on your phone call, but don't call 10 times a day. Financial aid administrators are meticulous people who don't forget to call back; they are simply overwhelmed with requests and oftentimes have hundreds of phone calls to return. Be patient.

- Cross you fingers!

I'm sure that my colleagues in financial aid would rather I not share this advice with you. However, I can't do that. You have to take your best interests to heart and to omit this critical step in the financial aid process would not serve your needs.

Chapter 7

Other Opportunities

T his chapter will present several other options to paying that tuition bill. You might be surprised by some of the opportunities and incentives offered by the government or some schools.

Tax incentives

Between federal and state taxes, most of you end up missing at least 33 percent of your gross income. In August of 1997, the Taxpayer Relief Act of 1997 was signed into law. The benefits of this new law include education tax credits, an education IRA, penalty-free withdrawals from traditional IRAs for education expenses, and a deduction for student loan interest. The following information will help you determine which benefits apply to you and your family.

Hope Scholarship

During the first two years of postsecondary education, students or parents may be able to take advantage of the Hope Scholarship tax credit. The credit can be as much as $1,500 per student per year for tuition and related expenses paid after December 31, 1997.

The tax credit will equal 100 percent of the first $1,000 of tuition and fees required for enrollment and attendance (not room or board) and 50 percent of the next $1,000 paid during the applicable tax year to an institution that participates in the U.S. Department of Education student aid programs.

To qualify, the student must have earned a high school diploma or equivalent degree, be enrolled at least half-time for one academic period during the tax year, and must not have been convicted of a federal or state drug felony.

The Hope Scholarship is available to individuals with a modified Adjusted Gross Income (AGI) under $40,000. For individuals, the credit is phased out for AGIs between $40,000 and $50,000. The credit is also available to joint filers with AGIs under $80,000 with the credit phased out for AGIs between $80,000 and $100,000.

Eligible family members include the taxpayer, the taxpayer's spouse, and the taxpayer's dependent(s).

Expenses paid after December 31, 1997 for education/ academic periods beginning in 1998 may be eligible. You cannot combine the Hope Scholarship credit with the Lifetime Learning credit or the Education IRA in the same year for the same child.

For example, a joint filing family with a modified AGI of $50,000 has a child attending college for the academic period of September 1999 through December 1999. Financial aid covers some of the tuition and fees, but leaves an uncovered balance of $3,000. One hundred percent of the first

$1,000 of out-of-pocket expenses and up to 50 percent of the remainder. In this scenario, the family would be eligible for the maximum Hope Scholarship credit of $1,500.

Lifetime Learning Tax Credit

Taxpayers can receive a tax credit up to $5,000 through the year 2002 (maximum annual credit of $1,000) and up to $10,000 beginning after 2002 (maximum annual credit of $2,000) for qualified tuition and expenses.

Expenses that qualify are tuition and fees for under-graduate, graduate, or professional degree courses for students enrolled at least half-time in a degree or certificate program. Tuition and fees for courses at an accredited institution to acquire or improve job skills are also eligible, even if the student is enrolled on a less than half-time basis.

Lifetime Learning credit is available to individuals with modified Adjusted Gross Income up to $40,000. The credit is phased out for AGIs between $40,000 and $50,000. Joint filers can receive the credit with AGIs up to $80,000. The credit is phased out for AGIs between $80,000 and $100,000.

Eligible family members include the taxpayer, the taxpayer's spouse, and the taxpayer's dependent(s).

Educational expenses paid after June 30, 1998, for an academic period after that date are eligible for credit for an unlimited number of tax years. You cannot combine the Lifetime Learning tax credit with the Hope Scholarship credit or the Education IRA in the same year for the same child.

For example: A college junior is attending full-time for the academic period September 1999 through December 1999. The family has an AGI of $25,000. After financial aid is applied, there is still a remaining obligation to the family of $5,000 for tuition and fees. The student meets all of the Lifetime Learning tax credit eligibility requirements and can expect to receive the maximum 1999 credit of $1,000.

IRA withdrawals

IRA withdrawals taken before age 59 1/2 (considered early withdrawals) are now allowed without penalty if the funds are withdrawn for education expenses for academic periods beginning on or after January 1, 1998. There are no income requirements and IRA withdrawals may be used for yourself, your spouse, your child, or grandchild.

For example: The parents of a college freshman have been contributing to a traditional IRA for a number of years. Their student's financial aid package covered all but $3,000 of the cost of tuition and fees for the academic period of September 1999 through December 1999. The parent taxpayers (age 45) may withdraw money from their IRA to cover the tuition fees, including room and board, without being assessed the 10 percent early withdrawal penalty. However, the distribution will still be taxed at the parent's tax rate.

Education IRAs

Qualified taxpayers will be able to establish Education IRAs and contribute up to $500 nondeductible per calendar year for each designated beneficiary under age 18. The beneficiary need not be your dependent child.

IRA withdrawals are tax-free and penalty-free, as long as the money is used for qualified education expenses. The Education IRA contribution maximum of $500 per year is in addition to the current $2,000 annual standard or Roth IRA contribution amount. You may not contribute to an Education IRA if, during the same tax year, you have made contributions to a qualified state prepaid tuition program for the same beneficiary.

Education IRAs are available for individuals with modified AGI under $95,000 and are phased out between $95,000 and $110,000. The Education IRA is available for joint filers with modified AGI under $150,000 and is phased out between $150,000 and $160,000.

You may make contributions to Education IRAs for tax years beginning January 1, 1998. You cannot combine the Education IRA with the Hope Scholarship credit or Lifetime Learning tax credit in the same year for the same child.

Student loan interest deduction

Qualified individuals are able to deduct a portion of their education loan interest up to $1,000 in 1998; $1,500 in 1999; $2,000 in 2000; and $2,500 in 2001 and after. Interest paid during the first 60 months (5 years) of scheduled repayment may be deductible. Deductions for student loan interest may be made for interest due and paid after 1997.

The tax credit is available for individuals with modified AGI under $40,000 and is phased out between $40,000 and $55,000. Joint filers with modified AGI under $60,000 are eligible for the deduction as well; it is phased out between $60,000 and $75,000.

Other opportunities

Prepaid tuition plans

Some colleges offer you the opportunity to pay for your student's college education up front. By doing so, you lock in the tuition rate of the academic year in which you pay for the student's entire college education. For a school that costs $10,000 per year to attend, the savings by paying up front can be as much as $1,576.25 assuming a 5 percent increase in tuition per year. Furthermore, inflation alone factors into the increasing costs of college. Paying tuition up front eliminates this factor. Some schools offer plans that can be paid in several installments in the years prior to enrollment. Check with your school to see if they offer such a program.

States also offer prepaid tuition plans. You can pay all in advance or some in installments. Prepaid tuition guarantees that you will at least cover the costs of college in the state of your residence. States are willing to gamble that, by investing your prepayment, their investments will outpace the rising cost of tuition.

Should your student decide to enroll in a school in another state, you can still use the funds; however, they may not meet all of your costs. The tuition plans include savings bond programs, savings funds, and savings plan trusts. Contact your state treasurer's office to learn whether such programs exist in your area.

College savings plans

Most state governments offer college savings plans. A family can contribute up to the state set maximum each year to these plans. Usually anyone interested in investing in a child's education can contribute. Better yet, in most cases, contributions to these plans are free of state tax. Earnings on the plans are also free from taxation. You have to start saving early to maximize your benefit. For more information, contact your state treasurer's office. I also recommend visiting *www.collegesavings.org*.

UGMAs/UTMAs

There are many ways to help our children as they journey toward adulthood. One way to do this is to invest on behalf of your child for the future. Putting money away for your child's future can help offset such costs as meeting college tuition costs, buying a home or car, or starting a family.

The Uniform Gift to Minors Act (UGMA) and Uniform Transfers to Minors Act (UTMA) rules were created through state laws that define special types of accounts and were designed to make giving to your children easy.

Under UGMA and UTMA provisions, your minor child is the owner of securities, but you may act as the custodian of the child's account. You can therefore prudently manage the securities that you have given to the minor until he or she reaches the age of majority. If you, as the grantor of the securities, also serve as the custodian, the assets involved will be included in your gross estate if you pass away prior to termination of the custodianship. Consult your tax advisor to determine the age for the termination of the custodianship in your UGMA or UTMA giving. (This may vary from state to state but it is usually 18 or 21.)

UGMA and UTMA custodianships operate under state laws in ways that are similar to trusts, without the complex agreements required by trusts. Equally important, passing ownership of assets to a minor in accordance with UGMA and UTMA allows some or all of the unearned income (such as dividends, interest, and capital gains) generated by assets you give to be taxed at the child's lower rate.

These securities are generally exempt from gift tax, up to the donor's $10,000 per donee annual exclusion for present interests and up to $20,000 for securities given jointly by spouses.

Income cutoffs

Why are so many investors choosing to open accounts for children in accordance with UGMA and UTMA? Because the potential tax savings can be significant, thanks to the difference between income tax brackets for adults and minors.

The first $700 (this amount varies and is adjusted for inflation annually) of unearned income in a minor's account is exempt from tax—regardless of his or her age.

The second $700 (this amount varies and is adjusted for inflation annually) of unearned income from securities given to a child is taxed according to the minor's tax bracket again, regardless of the minor's age. The child's age becomes a factor only when unearned income exceeds $1,400. If the minor is younger than 14 years of age at the close of the tax year, investment income over $1,400 is taxed at the parent's highest marginal rate.

Such income must be included on either a separate return or the parent's return. Because certain deductions may be available only to the child, filing a separate return for this income may result in a lower tax liability. If the minor reaches the age of 14 at any time during the year, all income in excess of $700 is taxed at the minor's rate, regardless of the parent's tax rate.

For the first $1,400 of investment income, a significant tax advantage can result from transferring securities to children provided those securities generate up to $1,400 of unearned income. For example, the maximum annual savings on unearned income of $1,400 would be:

$266   if the giving adult is in the 28 percent tax bracket

$305   for the 31 percent bracket

$370   for the 36 percent bracket

$417   for the 39.6 percent bracket

Similar savings would continue as income increases, so long as the child is age 14 or over and remains in a lower bracket than the parents.

Generally, investment income above $1,400 that is generated by securities given to children under age 14 will not provide you with income tax advantages. This income will be taxed at the parent's rate, regardless of who gives the securities to the child. Children who have either reached age 14 or will reach age 14 during the tax year usually will have additional tax savings available.

For 1997, the upper limit of the 15 percent bracket for single individuals like your child is reached when total taxable income from any source generating $24,650 of income is transferred to the child, saving a giving adult who is in the 28 percent bracket an additional $3,205 per year in taxes. Any income above that amount would put the child into the 28 percent bracket, which may produce additional tax savings if it prevents parents from moving into a higher bracket.

Please remember that these tax savings are available only if the assets are irrevocably transferred to the child, and that there may be gift tax consequences as discussed previously. Most important, please consult with your attorney and/or tax advisor before making any tax-related investment decisions.

One final note: Because the UGMA or UTMA account is the property of your child, you must list its value in the asset section for the student on the Free Application for Federal Student Aid (FAFSA). Keep in mind that 35 percent of a student's assets go directly toward the Expected Family Contribution calculated for your family. For example, if your child has $5,000 in an UGMA account, 35 percent or $1,750, will be expected to be used for education for the academic year in which you are applying for financial assistance.

Paying the bill

Paying bills is a fact of life. Paying tuition bills is pure torture. Seriously, college is an excellent investment. The 1992 U.S. Census demonstrated that a college graduate will earn 1.73 times as much during his or her lifetime as a high school graduate. Complete a master's program and earn 1.97 times as much as your high school graduate counterpart. If you are really ambitious, become a doctor, lawyer, or other professional and earn 3.67 times as much!

Okay, I know, it's overkill. I'm trying to make you feel better about shelling out the big bucks for college now. Here are some nuts and bolts involved in paying your bill.

Most colleges bill twice a year: once in July (due in August) and once in December (due in January). Some (if on trimester) bill three times a year. If you have sufficient funds, no problem—write a check.

However, if you need more time, there are other options. Some families choose to use a home equity line of credit to pay college expenses. Others opt to borrow using the Parent Loan for Undergraduate Students (PLUS). Still others choose alternative education loans. Colleges also (for the most part) offer time payment plans. For example, instead of paying the bill in two (roughly) equal payments, by using a payment plan you could spread those payments over 10 to 12 months.

So what option should you choose? The short answer is that it depends on your needs and ability to pay. Following is an overview of the options families use to meet the costs of college.

Home equity

Home equity loans are often tax deductible, carry competitive interest rates, and have reasonable repayment terms. They are also not my line of expertise. If you are considering an equity line of credit, be sure to consult your financial advisor or accountant to make sure this is a good choice for you.

If you choose the **Parent Loan for Undergraduate Students (PLUS)**, you can spread payments out over 10 years. The PLUS is a variable interest rate loan with a cap of 9 percent. The PLUS, as its name implies, is a loan that is taken in the name of a *parent*. The borrower (parent) may apply for as much as the student's cost of attendance minus financial aid. If you are uncertain about how much you can borrow or need to borrow, contact your student's financial aid office for a helping hand. You can prepay without penalty. So, if you don't need 10 years to repay, you can simply pay more than your monthly minimum. Keep in mind that the PLUS is not deferrable while the student is in school. Payments usually begin 60 days after the first disbursement of the loan.

Alternative loans

An alternative educational loan is borrowed in the name of the *student*. Most students are required to have a credit-worthy United States cosigner. A cosigner agrees to be financially liable for the loan should the student become unable to meet his/her payment obligations. Cosigners beware: If a student becomes delinquent, *your* credit report will suffer. Some alternative loans allow for the release of the cosigner after the student has made 48 consecutive on-time payments.

If you use an alternative loan to finance education, you may be able to defer payment up to four years. The catch is, you will either have to make interest-only payments or allow the interest to be capitalized. What does that mean for you? Capitalization means that the interest charged on the loan is added to the principal. Capitalization occurs at regular intervals throughout the year. The problem with capitalization is compounding interest. That means that, over time, interest is charged on interest. If you are able to, choose an alternative loan that capitalizes interest infrequently. Banks generally capitalize quarterly. Doing so will save you money over the long haul. And don't get mired in the interest rate charged on the loan. A loan with an interest rate 1 percent higher than another only amounts to a few dollars more come repayment time.

Payment plans

Payment plans are another fun way to meet your expenses and are vastly less complicated than loans! Schools generally use third parties to administer their plans. You pay an application fee — anywhere from $40 to $150 — and make regular payments to the school's payment plan administrator. In turn, the plan administrator pays the school. It's basically an escrow account. One attractive benefit of using a payment plan is that they often feature unemployment insurance and will continue to make your payments should you lose your job.

Conclusion

I n summary, there are many ways to pay for school. How you do so is basically a function of your own needs and the needs of your family. Choose the options that best meet your needs and push you or your student to excel. The fruits of this investment will pay for themselves many times over during the course of a lifetime!

Financial Aid Resources on the Web

Millions of families have access to the Internet. Whether it's at home, work, school, or the public library, you need to use the Internet to examine all aspects of your educational needs. Of course, one of the most immediate topics to consider is financial aid. There are a number of reputable providers of information on the Internet today. Best of all, it can be attained at no cost to you! On the following pages you will find my definitive guide to the must-see Web sites for financial aid information on the Internet.

Financial Aid Resource Center
www.theoldschool.org

A simply outstanding guide to financial aid—the best on the Internet. Shawn Lindstrom, a financial aid administrator, provides loads of great information on the entire financial aid process in a clear and easily understood fashion. Get on his free e-mail newsletter list!

FastAiD FREE Scholarship Search
www.fastaid.com

The world's largest and oldest private sector scholarship database. You will find scholarships here that you won't find anywhere else. The material is the result of 20 years of scholarship research, and it's constantly updated.

FreSch! The Free Scholarship Search Service!
www.freschinfo.com

This is an online database of thousands of sources of scholarships, searchable for free. The site also features tips on applying and well-moderated discussion forums. This site is outstanding.

The Student Guide to Financial Aid from the Department of Education
www.ed.gov/prog_info/SFA/StudentGuide

The ultimate source of information on financial aid from the federal government. An absolute must-read for every student and parent heading towards college!

FAFSA on The Web
www.fafsa.ed.gov

All students who want to take advantage of federal financial aid programs must file the Free Application for Federal Student Aid (FAFSA). Do it online and save time.

College Savings Plan Network
www.collegesavings.org

Find out what college savings programs are available in your state.

Appendix B

Helpful Publications

I have collected for quick reference some information on various publications, ranging from books to pamphlets published by a variety of sources. Topics covered include financial aid, college directories, handling college financial issues, or job selection. Each entry includes the name of the publication, address where you can send for information or the publication, the price, and a brief description.

Academic Year Abroad

Author: Sara J. Steen, Editor
Institute of International Education
IIE Books
809 United Nations Plaza
New York, NY 10017-3580

Cost: $44.95 plus $5 handling.

Provides information on more than 2,350 postsecondary study programs outside the United States.

AFL-CIO Guide to Union Sponsored Scholarships

Author: AFL-CIO Dept. of Education
AFL-CIO
815 16th St. NW
Washington, DC 20006

Cost: Free to union members; $3 to non-members.

Comprehensive guide for union members and their dependent children. Describes local, national, and international union-sponsored scholarship programs.

The Book (For Getting Out of Debt & Student Loans!)

1772 Piner Rd.
Suite 140
Santa Rosa, CA 95403
(707)569-1689

Cost: $29.95 plus $5 handling.

Guides you through the process of cleaning up your credit and getting out of debt, including student loan forgiveness. Easy to follow and simple to do. A booklet that can be used throughout your entire life.

The CARE Book (College Aid Resources for Education)
Author: Dr. Herm Davis
NCSF
16728 Frontenac Terr.
Rockville, MD 20855
(301)548-9423

Cost: $29.95.

Hands-on daily reference for counselors and families. Assists in finding statistics on colleges and comparing college costs, enrollments, form requirements, etc. Includes a CD-ROM money planner.

Career Materials Catalog
Author: CFKR
CFKR Career Materials Inc.
11860 Kemper Rd.
Unit 7
Auburn, CA 95603
(800)525-5626

Cost: free.

A catalog of printed materials, software, and videotapes covering career planning, college financing, and college test preparation. Includes materials applicable to all ages—from primary grades through graduate school.

Chronicle Four-Year College Databank
Author: CGP
Chronicle Guidance Publications
66 Aurora St.
P.O. Box 1190
Moravia, NY 13118-1190
(800)622-7284

Cost: $22.49 plus $2.25 handling. (Order No. 502CM4).

Reference book lists 2,160 institutions offering 760 four-year graduate and professional majors. Contains information and statistics on each of the schools.

Chronicle Two-Year College Databank
Author: CGP
Chronicle Guidance Publications
66 Aurora St.
P.O. Box 1190
Moravia, NY 13118-1190
(800)622-7284

Cost: $22.46 plus $2.25 handling (Order No. 502CM2).

Reference book lists 2,432 institutions offering 760 certificate/diploma, associate, and transfer programs. Contains information and statistics on each institution.

College Degrees by Mail
Author: John Bear, Ph.D.
Ten Speed Press
Box 7123
Berkeley, CA 94707
(510)845-8414

Cost: $12.95 plus $2.50 handling.

Listing of 100 colleges that offer B.A., M.A., Ph.D. and J.D. degrees by home study.

College Financial Aid Emergency Kit
Author: Joyce Lain Kennedy, et al.
Sun Features, Inc.
Box 368 (Kit)
Cardiff, CA 92007
(760)431-1660

Cost: $6.95.
40-page booklet filled with tips on how to meet the costs of college.

College Financial Aid for Dummies
Authors: Dr. Herm Davis and Joyce Lain Kennedy
Hastings Communications
P.O. Box 14927
Santa Rosa, CA 95402
(800)762-2974

Cost: $19.95.
The authors suggest "great ways to pay without going broke." For high school and college students and adults returning to school.

College Smarts — The Official Freshman Handbook
Author: Joyce Slayton Mitchell
Garrett Park Press
P.O. Box 190F
Garrett Park, MD 20896
(301)946-2553

Cost: $10.95.
Cogent advice for the college freshman. Covers such practical subjects as what things to take, coping with dorm life and your roommate, registration, fraternity/sorority rush, even your laundry.

Cooperative Education College Roster
Author: NCCE
National Commission for Cooperative Education
360 Huntington Ave.
384CP
Boston, MA 02115-5096
(617)373-3770

Cost: Free.

Explains what co-op education is, details its advantages, and lists colleges and universities that offer co-op education programs.

Dan Cassidy's Guide to Private Sector Kindergarten-12th Grade (K-12) Scholarships
5577 Skylane Blvd.
Suite 6A
Santa Rosa, CA 95403
(707)546-6777

Cost: $20.

90-page booklet of scholarships for elementary and secondary private schools with introduction on how to apply.

Dan Cassidy's Guide to Travel Grants
5577 Skylane Blvd.
Suite 6A
Santa Rosa, CA 95403
(707)546-6777

Cost: $20.

80-page booklet containing hundreds of sources of funding for travel in various fields of study and professions.

Dan Cassidy's Worldwide College Scholarship Directory, Fifth Edition
The Career Press, Inc.
P.O. Box 687
Franklin Lakes, NJ 07417
(800)227-3371

Cost: $23.99.

600-page listing of thousands of America's top undergraduate scholarships, grants, and awards, plus thousands more from 75 countries around the world.

Dan Cassidy's Worldwide Graduate Scholarship Directory, Fifth Edition
The Career Press, Inc.
P.O. Box 687
Franklin Lakes, NJ 07417
(800)227-3371

Cost: $26.99.

600-page listing of scholarships, grants, loans, fellowships, and internships from colleges, foundations, corporations, trust funds, associations, religious and fraternal groups, and private philanthropists for graduate and professional study.

Debt-Free Graduate
Author: Murray Baker
The Career Press, Inc.
P.O. Box 687
Franklin Lakes, NJ 07417
(800)227-3371

Cost: $13.99.

This money-management guide tells students how to stay out of debt and minimize costs while in college.

Directory of Financial Aids for Women
Author: Gail Ann Schlachter
Reference Service Press
5000 Windplay Dr.
Suite 4
El Dorado Hills, CA 95762
(415)594-0743

Cost: $45 plus $4 handling.

Contains information on more than 1,500 scholarships, fellowships, etc., set aside for women.

Dollars for College (Quick guides to financial aid in
several subject areas)
Garrett Park Press
P.O. Box 190
Garrett Park, MD 20896
(301)946-2553

Cost: $7.95 each; $60 for complete set of 12. Add $1.50 for
shipping regardless of order amount.

A series of 12 booklets on specific subject areas. 300 to 400-plus programs listed for each subject area.

Federal Benefits for Veterans & Dependents
Author: Veterans Administration
Superintendent of Documents
U.S. Government Printing Office
Washington, DC 20402

Cost: $5.50.

94-page booklet containing details of all federal benefit programs available to veterans and their dependents.

Financial Aid for Minorities
Garrett Park Press
P.O. Box 190F
Garrett Park, MD 20896

Cost: $5.95 each.

Several booklets with hundreds of sources of financial aid for minorities. When ordering, please specify which booklet: *Any Major; Business and Law; Education; Journalism and Mass Communications; Health; Engineering and Science.*

Financial Aid for the Disabled and Their Families
Author: Gail Ann Schlachter
Reference Service Press
5000 Windplay Dr.
Suite 4
El Dorado Hills, CA 95762
(415)594-0743

Cost: $38.50 plus $4 handling.

Contains financial aid information for the disabled and their families.

Finding Money for College
Author: John Bear, Ph.D.
Ten Speed Press
P.O. Box 7123
Berkeley, CA 94707
(510)845-8414

Cost: $8.95 plus $3.50 handling.

Lists the unconventional, overlooked, and not well-understood sources of assistance and how to pursue them.

Fly Bucks
Author: Daniel J. Cassidy
5577 Skylane Blvd.
Suite 6A
Santa Rosa, CA 95403
(707)546-6777

Cost: $20.

30-page booklet containing more than 80 sources of funding for education in aeronautics, aviation, aviation electronics, aviation writing, space science, aviation maintenance technology, and vertical flight.

How to Win a Sports Scholarship
Authors: Penny Hastings and Todd D. Caven
First Base Sports, Inc.
P.O. Box 1731-N
Manhattan Beach, CA 90267-1731
(800)684-6845

Cost: $19.95.

Provides a step-by-step approach to attracting more than 150,000 athletic scholarships worth more than $600 million annually in fields ranging from archery to wrestling.

International Jobs
Author: Eric Kocher
Perseus Books
1 Jacob Way
Reading, MA 01867

Cost: $16.
Career opportunities around the world.

Making It Through College
Author: PSC
Professional Staff Congress
25 West 43rd St.
5th Floor
New York, NY 10036

Cost: $1.

Handy booklet describing some of the ups and downs of college and everything in between and how to make it through.

Music Scholarship Guide (Third Edition)
Author: Sandra V. Fridy
Music Educators National Conference
1806 Robert Fulton Dr.
Reston, VA 20191

Cost: $33 ($26.40 MENC members).

Lists more than 2,000 undergraduate music scholarships in more than 600 public and private educational institutions in the United States and Canada; includes eligibility requirements, application deadlines, and contact information.

National Directory of College Athletics
(Men's and Women's Editions)
Author: Kevin Cleary, Editor/Publisher
Collegiate Directories, Inc.
P.O. Box 450640
Cleveland, OH 44145

Cost: $29.95 (men's edition); $23.95 (women's edition).

Comprehensive directory of college athletic programs in the United States and Canada. Revised for each new school year.

Need a Lift?
Author: American Legion
Attn: National Emblem Sales
P.O. Box 1055
Indianapolis, IN 46206
(317)630-1200

Cost: $3.

Guide to education and employment opportunities, as well
as the financial aid process.

Occupational Outlook Handbook
Author: U.S. Bureau of Labor Statistics
CFKR Career Materials
11860 Kemper Rd.
Unit 7
Auburn, CA 95603
(800)525-5626

Cost: $16.95.

Annual publication designed to assist in selecting careers.
Describes approximately 250 occupations.

Off to College
Author: Guidance Research Group
Order Fulfillment Dept-98-RSCH
P.O. Box 931
Montgomery, AL 36101

Cost: $3.

Helps prepare incoming freshmen for success in college.

Peterson's Colleges with Programs for Students with Learning Disabilities and A.D.D. (Fifth Edition)
Peterson's, Inc.
P.O. Box 2123
Princeton, NJ 08543-2123
(800)225-0261

Cost: $32.95.

Comprehensive guide to more than 1,000 two-year and four-year colleges and universities offering special academic programs for students with dyslexia and other learning disabilities.

Peterson's Guide to Four-Year Colleges
Peterson's, Inc.
P.O. Box 2123
Princeton, NJ 08543-2123
(800)225-0261

Cost: $24.95.

Profiles more than 1,900 colleges in the United States and Canada.

The Scholarship Book 2000
Author: Dan Cassidy
NSRS
5577 Skylane Blvd., #6A
Santa Rosa, CA 95403

Cost: $37.68 (includes tax and shipping; add $11.83 for hardbound).

Identifies more than 400,000 awards worth $2 billion in scholarships, grants, and loans.

Student Guide—Financial Aid from the U.S. Department of Education
Author: U.S. Department of Education
Federal Student Aid Information Center
P.O. Box 84
Washington, DC 20044
(800)4-FEDAID

Cost: Free.

Lists qualifications and sources of information for federal grants, loans, and work-study programs.

Study Abroad
United Nations Educational,
Scientific, and Cultural Organization
Bernan Associates
UNESCO Agent U7154
4611-F Assembly Dr.
Lanham, MD 20706

Cost: $29.95 plus handling.

Lists 3,700 international study programs.

Vacation Study Abroad
Author: Sara J. Steen, Editor
Institute of International Education
IIE Books
809 United Nations Plaza
New York, NY 10017-3580

Cost: $39.95 plus $5 handling.

Guide to 1,800 study abroad programs.

What Color Is Your Parachute?
Author: Richard N. Bolles
Ten Speed Press
P.O. Box 7123
Berkeley, CA 94707
(800)841-BOOK

Cost: $16.95 plus $4.50 handling.
Career planning guide, with tips on job hunting and changing careers.

Winning Scholarships For College
Author: Marianne N. Ragins
The Scholarship Workshop
P.O. Box 6845
Macon, GA 31208
(912)755-8428

Cost: $13.95.
Author recounts how she received more than $400,000 in tuition money.

National Totals for All Financial Aid Sources

Financial Aid Sources	Amounts Awarded in Billions				% of Total
Private Scholarships & Fellowships Controlled & awarded by the private sector [1]			30.10		39.34
Private Scholarships & Fellowships Controlled & awarded by schools [2]			13.14		17.17
Public institutions	5.09				
Private Institutions	8.05				
Total Private Financial Aid Funding			43.24		
Percentage of Private Financial Aid Funding					56.51
Federal Programs [3] generally available aid					
Pell Grants	5.68				
Specially-directed aid	2.24				
Other	5.90				
Subtotal of Federal Aid [4]			13.82		18.06
Stafford Student Loans		14.12			
Supplemental Loans for Students		3.48			
Subtotal of Federal Loan Programs			17.60		23.00
<<<*Note: 56% of the federal funding is loans*>>>					
Total Federal Aid			31.42		41.06
State Grant Programs [5]			1.86		2.43
Total Government Financial Aid Funding			33.28		
Percentage of Total Federal Aid					43.49
Total Private & Public Financial Aid Funding				76.52	

(1) Source: Database survey, National Scholarship Research Service, December 1991. This survey result is independently corroborated by data reported in *Foundation Giving* (New York: The Foundation Center, 1994), p. 10 and in *The Chronicle of Philanthropy* (April 1990) from which we calculate that $24.907 billion in financial aid is available from the private sector based on reports that, on average, 15 percent of philanthropic giving is devoted to scholarships, fellowships, grants and other moneys for postsecondary education. See *Cassidy Endowment for Education Reports: Growth in Philanthropy and Scholarships 1982-1993*.

(2) Source: *The Digest of Education Statistics 1995* (US Department of Education, National Center for Education Statistics, Office of Educational Research and Improvement), p. 327, table 315. Figures are for the academic year 1992-1993.

(3) Source: *The Chronicle of Higher Education, Almanac Issue* (1 September 1995), p. 37. Figures are for academic year 1993-1994.

(4) Source: *The Chronicle of Higher Education, Almanac Issue* (1 September 1995), p. 37. Figures are for academic year 1993-1994.

(5) Source: *The Chronicle of Higher Education, Almanac Issue* (1 September 1995), p. 37. Figures are for academic year 1993-1994.

About the NSRS

I f you would like to receive a brochure describing National Scholarship Research Service's computerized scholarship search service, an application form, or any of a number of materials on financial aid we offer, call (800)432-3782, or write to:

National Scholarship Research Service
5577 Skylane Blvd., Ste. 6A,
Santa Rosa, CA 95403

🕐🕐🕐

The Cassidy Endowment for Education (CEE), a public benefit non-profit organization, is pleased to announce this year that it will be providing scholarships for graduate students. Please call (707)546-6898 for an application, or contact the Web site at *www.gradstudies.com*.

If you need help in starting or managing a scholarship, or would just like to donate to the Cassidy Endowment for Education's scholarship program, please phone or write:

Cassidy Endowment for Education (CEE)
5577 Skylane Blvd.; Ste. 6A
Santa Rosa, CA 95403
Phone: (707)546-6898
Fax: (707)546-6897
E-mail: dcassidy@fastap.org

Index

BRIGHTON

BRIGHTON

LB 2337.4 .C396 2000
Cassidy, Daniel J., 1956-
Last minute college
  financing

NOV 2 8 2000

19